HUNGER

MELVIN BURGESS

HAMMER

AN EXCLUSIVE MEDIA COMPANY

Published by Arrow Books in association with Hammer 2013

2 4 6 8 10 9 7 5 3 1

First published in Great Britain in 2013 by
Arrow Books in association with Hammer
The Random House Group Limited
20 Vauxhall Bridge Road,
London SW1V 2SA

www.randomhouse.co.uk

Addresses for companies within The Random House Group Limited can be found at:
www.randomhouse.co.uk/offices.htm

The Random House Group Limited Reg. No. 954009

A CIP catalogue record for this book
is available from the British Library

ISBN 9780099576648

The Random House Group Limited supports The Forest Stewardship Council
(FSC®), the leading international forest certification organisation. Our books
carrying the FSC label are printed on FSC® certified paper. FSC is the only forest
ce   nisations,
                                                                ound at:

HUNGER

By the same author

The Cry of the Wolf
An Angel for May
Burning Issy
The Baby and Fly Pie
Loving April
The Earth Giant
Junk
Tiger, Tiger
Kite
The Copper Treasure
Bloodtide
Old Bag
The Birdman
The Ghost Behind the Wall
Billy Elliot
Lady: My Life as a Bitch
Doing It
Robbers on the Road
Sara's Face
Bloodsong
Nicholas Dane
Kill All Enemies

To Dr Fell and all his little pets

HUNGER

Prologue

Beth knew that things had moved on when she awoke one morning to find dirt in her bed. It wasn't the fine soil that you might find in a bag of compost, but dirt from the ground, damp and gritty against her skin. She tried to sit up, but her back was crippled with pain as if she'd been labouring all night. But she had no memory of it. For a moment she thought she must still be asleep, dreaming, but from downstairs came the ordinary sounds of the day, her housemates getting breakfast, muted voices and music on the radio.

The smell of toast crept into her room and she realised how hungry she was. She'd never been so hungry. It felt as if she hadn't eaten for a hundred years. She ran her hands down her body and found a worm flattened under her bottom. She picked it off, looked curiously at it, and ran her tongue round her mouth.

Grit.

She struggled upright. Her fingers stung. Both hands were covered with broken blisters and dried blood and her fingernails were black with dirt. Every muscle, every tendon in her was racked with pain and her skin was peppered with tiny dents from the little stones she had slept on.

Trying not to panic, Beth got out of bed and hobbled to the bathroom. What had she been doing? She had no memory of anything that could have left her feeling like this. She swilled her mouth at the tap and spat dirty water into the sink, then spent a couple of minutes swishing water between her teeth to make sure that every trace of grit had gone. She got into the shower and watched the dirt fall away from her, trying to remember. There was no memory at all. She snorted in exasperation, then soaped the flannel and scrubbed herself until her skin stung and the suds ran pure and white.

Chapter One

It was ten a.m. and people were already stirring — Beth's brother Louis and her best friend Coll, geeking away as usual, she thought crossly. Beth desperately needed to go down and get something to eat, but first she had to deal with her dirty bed. She stripped the mattress, hid the grimy sheets in a cupboard, put on her dressing gown and headed down for breakfast. She paused in the hallway to pull on a pair of thin leather gloves to hide the marks on her hands, then went to open the kitchen door. The reassuring smells of coffee and toast wafted over her and the hunger returned. It hit her so hard, she swayed on her feet.

Coll had already left, but Ivan and Louis were still around. Ivan smiled hopefully at her. She'd spent the night with him a couple of weeks ago and ever since he had been looking for a replay. Beth shook her head.

'You OK?' he asked. 'What's up with your hands?' he added, seeing the gloves.

'Nail-biting,' she lied. It was a habit she'd been fighting for years.

Ivan looked amused and glanced at Louis to see if it was worth a tease, but he had other things on his mind.

'What were you up to last night?' he asked. 'Couldn't you sleep?' he said when she didn't reply. 'It must have been four in the morning.'

'Girls' things,' said Beth. She sat herself down, trying to hide her stiffness, and helped herself to cereal. He'd seen her, then. She wanted to grab hold of him and demand – *What was I doing? How did I look?* She was a mystery to herself.

'Not girl and boy things?' Louis asked. He said it like it was a joke but she knew what he was up to. Ever since she'd moved in a few months ago, he'd become like some kind of surrogate dad. He liked Ivan, but disapproved of him – quite rightly, in some ways. Ivan was a lech. None of the girls in his own year would go anywhere near him, he was such soiled meat. But that was Beth's business, not her brother's. Louis had no idea that things had already gone as far as they had but ever since he'd caught them snogging at a house party a few weeks ago he had gone into protective overdrive.

He was fishing to see if she'd been in Ivan's room overnight.

Beth was infuriated. As if she didn't have enough going on without Louis poking his nose in where it wasn't wanted. 'What's it to you?' she snapped.

'Just taking a healthy interest,' he said defensively.

'In my sex life? What's healthy about that?'

'Sister sex,' said Ivan. 'It's not nice, but it has to happen. You should be encouraging her.'

Beth scowled. 'As if I'd do it with you,' she said.

Ivan looked shocked. She'd only said it to put Louis off the scent. She wanted to kiss him better, but hardened her heart.

'Sorry,' said Louis. He knew he ought to stop but couldn't help himself. 'You know what he's like.'

'Er, are we talking about me?' asked Ivan.

'Yes, exactly, Louis – I know what he's like. So how about letting me make my own decisions?'

Louis rolled his eyes but shut up. Beth finished her cereal and poured herself another bowl. She'd have got up to get a banana if she wasn't scared of hobbling. Louis watched her curiously as she wolfed it down.

'You can't give girls advice on this stuff,' Ivan was telling her brother. 'You've only slept with one girl in three years.'

'Idle speculation,' said Louis. 'Just because I don't boast. Just because,' he added significantly, 'I don't go to the bar straight afterwards and give girls ratings out of ten.'

There was a pause.

'You bastard,' said Ivan.

'Ratings out of ten for kissing and, er, hand skills, shall we say; and for—'

'That was in my first year,' said Ivan. He shook his head. 'I can't believe you said that. That was private information,' he fumed.

'I expect that's what those girls thought,' said Louis smugly, glancing at his sister.

Beth sighed. She knew this. She got another bowlful – her third. The boys rattled on. Soon Beth had finished her cereal and was wondering if she dared risk having another in front of the ever-watchful Louis when she caught a whiff of something foul.

'What's that smell?' she asked.

'What smell?' Louis sniffed the air. 'I can't smell anything.'

'Is it the bin?' she asked, turning towards it. She sniffed. It was rot all right. And then, without warning, the smell increased tenfold. It wasn't just a smell, it was a stench, a choking miasma. There was no mistaking it. It was the smell of rotting flesh – the stench of death.

Beth retched as it hit her throat. At the same moment

the hunger came rushing in on her again. She looked up guiltily. The boys were watching her curiously. It was obvious that they could smell nothing at all.

'You're eating too fast,' said Louis.

'What?'

'That was your third bowl. You're eating too fast. No wonder it's making you sick.'

'Fuck off, Louis,' she snapped. It gave her an excuse to run. She got up and stormed out as best she could, clutching hold of chairs and the doorknob to support herself on the way out.

Louis shook his head at the banging door behind her.

'What's up with her?'

'Dunno. Why?' asked Ivan, who hadn't noticed anything unusual.

'Did you see the way she walked?'

Ivan lifted up his hands. 'I never touched her,' he said.

'You're an idiot, Ivan,' said Louis absently. Something was going on. The chances were, he was going to be the last one to know what it was.

Upstairs, Beth wept. A pit of misery was opening up inside her. That disgusting smell – was it really there for her alone? How was it possible to eat three huge bowls of cereal and still feel famished? There was only one experience in her life she could compare this with; depression. When she had been fourteen, for reasons no one could fathom, it had come from nowhere, hauled her down into its grim bosom and kept her prisoner for half a year before she'd popped unaccountably and suddenly back to the surface. Was this it again, transformed in the intervening years into this terrifying monster that stole her nights and forced her to gorge like a dog?

As soon as Louis and Ivan left the house, she got out of bed and searched for clues. The clothes she had worn the day before were missing. She found them in the wardrobe, covered with dirt. Cautiously, she put her face to the bag that contained them and sniffed. It was just earth and clay – but where had it come from?

Beth continued her search. She found her boots, also filthy with mud, tucked under the bed. And a coat of hers was missing, a waterproof anorak. She searched the house from top to bottom but there was no trace of it anywhere. Back in her room, she flung herself down on her bed and tried to force the memories that must lie inside her to the surface. What had she done, where had she been? Concentrate, Beth!

She found it at last, that forgotten night, but like a

faded dream there were no real memories, only shadows. Darkness had blossomed inside her. It was not empty. On the contrary, it was brimming over with an ancient and insatiable greed that left her feeling desperate with the desire to feed.

This was no dream: it was a memory – but no memory that *she'd* ever had. What was someone else's memory doing inside her head?

She must have fallen asleep, because she was awoken again by Coll later that afternoon. 'You're such a little grub – look at you, sleeping without sheets. What's up?'

'I've been sick,' lied Beth. Coll pulled her into the desk chair in the corner of her room and nattered away about her morning as she bustled about making the bed. When she'd finished playing mum, she heaved her from the chair and tried to put her to bed, but Beth needed more food. She went down and made herself two cheese sandwiches, which she took back up to bed with half a packet of choc-chip biscuits, a banana and a glass of milk. Coll watched in horror.

'You're on a journey straight to obesity town, girl,' she told her, settling down on the bed. Beth pretended not to care. Coll was slim and tall, and Beth had always been on the dumpy side. She sat miserably next to her, friend, feeling squat and ugly, mopping up crumbs from her plate with a finger while Coll watched her anxiously. Louis had mentioned that she'd been a bit funny that morning.

'Feeling a bit down in the dumps, are you?' Coll asked. Beth grimaced and shook her head. 'Not now, babe,' said Coll. 'This is our first year at uni.' She paused a moment, wondering if she'd said the wrong thing. She usually had. 'Is it happening again?' she asked.

'I don't know,' said Beth.

'If it does, don't you dare shut me out this time,' demanded Coll.

'I'm not down,' insisted Beth. Then she rocked in her seat as an unbidden thought struck her. What was happening to her was not a lessening of herself but a completion. She was turning into what she was always meant to me: some kind of monster. This idea terrified her.

'. . . panic attack . . .' Beyond her confusion, someone was speaking.

'What?'

'You're having a panic attack.' Coll was reaching out to her but Beth pushed her away. She became aware that she was panting. 'Breathe slowly,' Coll was saying. 'Hey. It's OK, Bethie. Breathe.'

'I'm OK,' insisted Beth, forcing herself to speak evenly. But it was obviously not true.

Coll waited while she got herself under control. 'How long have you been feeling like this?' she asked.

Beth looked away, unable to bring herself to talk about it. 'I'm OK,' she said again. Coll shook her head. 'Just today,' Beth admitted finally. 'Don't tell Louis,' she begged. 'You know what he's like. I'll never hear the end of it.' Unable to hold it together any longer, she began to cry.

'Oh, Bethie,' said Coll. She grabbed hold of her and hugged her tight. 'Just don't hide it away this time. Promise me. OK?'

But Beth could not promise anything. She just clung to her like a child and wept.

They went way back a long way, these two, all the way to their first year at high school; the tall blonde one and the short dark one, ever since Coll, with braces on her teeth and her skirt rolled up at the waist to reveal far too much of her skinny legs, had walked up and asked Beth if she really was Louis Middleton's sister.

Beth looked askance at her and cautiously admitted that yes, she might be.

'Great. Let's be friends. I'm going to go out with him when I'm older,' Coll said brightly.

Beth looked at her and sighed. An oddball herself,

she had no intention of having another oddball as a friend. But Coll stuck to her like glue and before she knew it, friends they were and friends they'd stayed — despite the fact that, so far, Coll's prophecy about Louis had failed to come true.

Coll petted her, and felt helpless. She was a competent person, intelligent, confident, used to knowing what she wanted and how to get it. But four years ago she had seen her friend collapse in on herself and had no idea what to do or how to help. Now it looked as though it was happening again. They were both four years older but Coll felt as helpless as ever.

'You're going to have to get some help, baby,' she said. 'You can't do it all on your own, you know? See someone. I'll come with you if you like.'

Beth shook her head. 'I'm not depressed. I'll be OK,' she said. 'Give me another few days, all right?'

Coll wasn't convinced. 'You're scaring me,' she said. 'Sorry.'

'Just remember, I'm here for you, Beth. You don't have to go through this stuff on your own.'

Beth dried her tears and Coll tried to cheer her up with one of her favourite themes — Louis. For the past couple of years he had been going out with a pretty Jewish girl called Samantha but last summer she'd dumped him and now he was back on the market. For Coll, it had become something of a challenge.

'He'd have taken you up on it by now,' insisted Beth. 'He's had enough chances.'

'But take into account I'm getting more gorgeous all the time,' Coll pointed out. 'He can't hold out for ever. No man could.'

Beth laughed. 'But what for? Everyone knows that Christians are no good at sex.'

'Not true. You need that sense of sin before you can get really filthy. Behind every cross,' pronounced Coll, 'there lurks a dirty mind.'

'You know that?'

'I've done the research.'

They chatted away for a while, but then Coll's foot bumped against something tucked under the bed, hidden by the duvet. It was a brick, covered in black earth, still wet from the underground. Beth's heart leaped in fright.

'What's this doing here?' Coll laughed nervously and glanced at her friend. Beth was staring at the brick as if it was a ghost. 'Look, there's something written on it.' She found a magazine and brushed the dirt onto it. 'Where did you get it?'

'In the garden. Yesterday,' Beth replied. She'd never seen it before in her life.

'Starting a brick collection. How novel,' said Coll

brightly. She brushed the dirt away with some tissues from her bag. 'It's Latin,' she announced.

Beth leaned over and studied the inscription. '*Pro fame perpetua*,' she read. 'What does it mean?' she asked.

'I don't know Latin. We didn't do it at school, worse luck.'

'Geek. You could have been lynched for even thinking that.'

'Geek is a word invented by the stupid to make them feel better about their own ignorance,' said Coll. She hefted the brick and looked anxiously at her friend again. 'It's not like you,' she observed, 'finding homes for stray masonry.'

'I thought my dad might be interested.'

Coll snorted. 'Your dad might be a builder but that doesn't make him interested in bricks,' she said. But the Latin interested her. 'Can I take it in to uni tomorrow? Find out what it says?'

Beth wouldn't let her. Coll had to write the inscription down and be content with that. She hung around a little longer, wanting to help but unable to get a handle on what was happening, before leaving to get on with her own afternoon. On her own, Beth stared at the brick, which lay maliciously silent on the magazine by her bed, another clue she did not know the answer to. She examined it carefully, held it in her hand, weighed it, sniffed it, stared at it, but it refused to tell her anything. In the end, she wrapped it in a plastic bag and tucked it back under the bed. She feared it, but for reasons she could not fathom, she was unwilling to let it go.

Beth spent the rest of the day hiding in her room. In the evening, her brother cooked chicken stew. The smell was irresistible, and she crept down to feed.

'I thought this might get you up,' said Louis. He gestured with the spoon at Ivan and Coll waiting at the table. 'The wolves have gathered.'

Beth smiled back – a little grimly, because she suspected that the chicken was for her, really; and who did he think he was, her bloody mother? And if she was depressed – and she bloody wasn't, not if she could help it – then of course food would be her first recourse. Last time she'd come out of it looking like Miss Bouncy Castle. No way was that going to happen again.

She sat down to join the others. Ivan smiled and offered her a beer; she smiled back and accepted it. Louis ladled out the stew. Helpless in her hunger, Beth had to force herself to eat it slowly.

'I'm going to miss this if you go veggie,' she told him. He'd been threatening to do that for ages. Louis nodded, pleased to be friends again. Beth ate till her stomach hurt, trying to ignore the sideways looks she was getting as she swallowed plateful after plateful, mopped up with thick slices of bread. She cleared up afterwards with Ivan and Coll. It was nice; it was normal. Beth did the washing-up, feeling ridiculously happy that she could still enjoy such stuff.

When Coll left the room to go to the loo, Ivan came up behind her and put his arms around her waist as she stood at the sink.

'What do you want?' she said.

'You know,' he told her, nuzzling.

Beth shook her head. She was just a bit too fond already, and Ivan was someone you simply couldn't trust.

'I was drunk,' she said.

'So was I.'

'You're always drunk.'

'I'm not drunk now.'

'You will be.'

He laughed. It was so true. Beth loved the way he laughed at himself so easily, but made herself push him away.

'You're such a lech. I'd rather just be friends,' she lied.

Ivan looked stricken. And she wished it was different, but she sent him away anyway. All those girls. How could you ever tell with someone like that, never knowing whether you were just another notch on the bedpost?

'So,' said Coll, when she came back in. 'I thought that was going to be a one-off?'

'Just doing a little research,' said Beth.

'Into what?'

'Sex, you dummy.'

'I thought *I* was supposed to be the geek,' said Coll.

'Being a sex geek I can handle.'

'Sex geek. Doesn't that involve wearing latex and having a wrinkly bottom?'

'Not in my case.'

They had a laugh. It was great. Beth felt so much better and when Coll asked how she felt she was able to honestly say that she was OK. Together, they finished the kitchen and went to join the boys next door.

They had the usual argument about what to watch and ended up with *Shaun of the Dead* for about the tenth time. It wasn't funny any more but Beth wanted something familiar. The first time she'd seen it was with her dad and her brother way back, and it carried fond memories. She caught Louis glancing at her and smiled back reassuringly. Louis relaxed and Beth allowed herself to think that maybe everything was going to be all right after all.

About halfway through the film she became aware

of a pressure behind her eyes. She rubbed them and watched the room sway in front of her – and then darkness began to leak into her from below. She clutched the cushion and tried to fight it but it was an irresistible tide, flooding rapidly up from deep inside her, impenetrable and poisonous. It was followed a moment later by an overwhelming stench of rotting meat. Shocked, she clamped her hand over her mouth and retched.

'You all right, babes?' asked Coll.

Beth nodded and then, without warning, vomited dinner, lunch, breakfast – the lot – all over the carpet. She slumped back on the sofa in a faint. Everyone jumped up, shocked and disgusted. Coll grabbed hold of her and hauled her upstairs to bed. She tucked her up, gave her water to drink, put a bowl by the bedside, and sat and stroked her head.

'There you go, babe – it's good news! You're just sick,' whispered Coll. Beth nodded. Let her think that. No one could ever know what she was like inside.

Coll stayed with her for a short while, then left. On her own, Beth lay still, trying to fight the bile in her throat. She was exhausted but too scared to sleep. Sleep, she knew, was not her friend. After a while, she sat up with her laptop and tried to work instead. As she waited for it to fire up, a cracked, dried voice called her name. It was so clear, she let out a little scream. She jumped up and locked the door. But that was foolish. What good was locking the door going to do, when the voice came from inside her?

'It's the wrong door,' she said out loud. And she had no idea where that thought came from, either, or what it meant. Where was the right door? How could you bar it, when it was inside you?

'Who are you?' she whispered. But there was no reply. She lay down, too tired to stay up, too scared to sleep. At some point in the night, maybe hours later for all she knew, her phone flashed its blue light at her. A text.

'The fast that will not stop,' she read.

Without thinking she texted back: 'For the dead, the hunger that never ends.'

Then she lay back down, fighting the hunger, the darkness, the stink, until sleep overcame her.

Chapter Two

In the morning, Beth's housemates looked in on her before they left. Ivan was very sweet and attentive, asking her if there was anything he could do and promising to come by again later. Louis hung about, looking suspicious or scared, she wasn't sure which. Coll came in last, and leaned across to hug her. 'Day in bed. Lucky cow,' she said.

Just to be sick. Beth would give anything just to be sick.

Coll sat back up. 'Hey, by the way, that translation was brilliant,' she told her. 'How did you work it out?'

'What?'

'"The hunger that never ends." Much better than my version.'

Beth had forgotten all about the text. It had been from Coll – a translation of the inscription on the brick. But she hadn't worked it out. She'd barely been awake. She just knew.

'Brilliant,' said Coll again. 'What did you do, run it through one of those translation engines? It must be a really good one.'

'What's this about bricks?' Louis wanted to know.

'Something I found in the garden. None of your business, actually,' snapped Beth.

Louis shrugged, looked hurt, and left. Coll looked warily at her friend. 'You're being really hard on him,' she said. 'He's just worried.'

'It's just a brick,' Beth said. 'I don't know why you're making such a fuss about it.' A suspicion grabbed her. 'Have you two been talking about me?' she complained.

Coll shrugged. 'Why wouldn't we?' she said. Beth didn't answer. 'Actually, your pet brick turns out to be pretty interesting,' Coll went on. 'Guess what – it's Roman! The shape is distinctive. I was checking it up last night. That brick might be nearly two thousand years old.'

'Is that how you spend your nights – researching bricks?' demanded Beth, trying to head her off.

'I was just relaxing after doing my history paper. But I haven't told you the best bit. You know that grave that got robbed?'

Beth's heart jumped. 'What grave?'

'Didn't you hear? At St Michael's in Withington. An unmarked burial. No one even knew it was there – it was outside the boundary wall, in a school playing field. Unsanctified ground. Some sinner or other. All the remains got taken away, but they left something behind – guess what? Some Roman jewellery! A man's ring. See? If you found that brick in our garden, that means there might actually be some Roman ruins, right here, under the ground, waiting to be dug up.' Coll beamed with pleasure. 'Roman archaeology, in our own back garden! Exciting or what?'

Coll rabbited on but Beth had stopped listening. A robbed grave. Dirt in her bed. Darkness. Hunger. It was too much of a coincidence. She thought about the brick, lying there all that time . . .

'Just think of it,' she said. 'Four hundred years of hunger . . .'

'What?' asked Coll. 'Where'd that come from?'

But Beth had no idea herself. 'The brick's been in the ground that long?' she suggested weakly.

'Babe, what's happening to you? You're turning into a poet. It's a brick. It doesn't do hungry.'

Beth had another visitor later, about midday – John, her dad. She was so pleased to see him, she leaped out of bed and hugged him, despite her sore muscles. The family home wasn't more than an hour or so away, but she'd seen nothing of him since she'd started uni. She hadn't been at all homesick so far, but now that he was here she realised how much she'd missed him.

'Did Louis tell you?' she asked, her happiness darkened by a sudden suspicion.

'No.' He smiled. 'Well, he told me, but I rang him. I was passing by, so . . .' He shrugged. 'Thought I'd see how you are.'

'Just passing by,' she parroted, disbelieving.

He settled himself down beside her and raised his eyebrows. 'Stomach bug?' he said. 'Louis said you weren't well.'

'I'm not sure,' she began. She stumbled over the words, but if she couldn't tell her father, who was there? Her mum had died years ago when she was only four. He and Louis were all she had. 'I think I might be walking in my sleep,' she said at last.

'OK.' John nodded calmly. 'What exactly have you been doing, do you know? Have you been talking as well?'

'I don't think so. Why?'

John waited a moment, thinking. 'You used to before. When you were little. You walked and talked in your sleep.'

This was news. 'You never said.'

He shrugged. 'It's a thing children sometimes do.'

'What did I do? What did I say?'

John looked at her. Despite his apparent calm, he didn't like this development with his daughter at all. Back then, the whole thing had been deeply disturbing. In fact, it had terrified him.

It had begun, as strange things tend to, with something ordinary: a child's dream. The circumstances were far from ordinary, though. It had first occurred just a few months after his wife, Beth's mother, had died of breast cancer. Beth was four years old at the time. He'd heard voices in her room and ran up to find her sitting up in bed. Her eyes were open but he'd known at once that she was fast asleep.

'I can't feel anything but at least I can move again,' she said suddenly. To John's terror, it was not her voice. She had an accent for one thing, and although it was using her breath, her throat, he was certain that the voice belonged to a man.

She grinned and licked her lips. 'This child is my gateway back to life,' she exclaimed. Panicked, John shook her but had to struggle to wake her. When he asked her what she had been dreaming of, and who

that man was, Beth looked at him anxiously. 'Someone not nice,' she said.

After that it was as if a door had opened. Over the
next few weeks a number of visitors appeared, some
male, some female. John assumed it was a disturbance
caused by the death of her mother and tried to wait
it out – but then things took a more disturbing turn.
She called to him late one night, again not with her
own voice. He ran up to find her sitting bolt upright
in bed.

'This child needs watching,' she exclaimed. He
tried to shake her awake again but she resisted.

'Don't push me away, don't make me go, she needs
me, John, she needs me,' cried the voice. But he
persisted until the little eyes focused. Beth awoke, and
began to cry.

John Middleton had been an atheist for most of
his life. His wife, Joan, had tried to convince him of
the existence of a loving God, but this was the first
time he had been forced to consider the possibility
that the journey from life to death was not a one-way
street. The voice in which Beth had spoken to him
was that of his dead wife. It was too much. John had
loved Joan deeply and this was breaking his heart all
over again. It had to stop. There followed doctors and
psychotherapists and counsellors. The medics were
of the opinion that, although undeniably odd, it was

an understandable way for a little girl to mourn her recently dead mother, and advised John to let things take their course. But he simply could not bear it. In the end he was directed to a therapist in Manchester who believed he could put an end to these episodes easily and harmlessly through hypnosis.

The night after the second session he was awoken from a deep sleep to find Beth standing by his bed.

'This is dangerous,' she told him. The voice was so clearly Joan's. John pulled himself upright. He muttered something about normal not being a very common commodity these days. Beth shook her head.

'She is extraordinary. I can help but you're shutting me out. Don't stop me, John – I won't have it. Do you hear me, John? She needs me.'

'You can wake up now, Beth,' said John.

'I haven't finished. I—'

'And what about the child?' insisted John quietly. 'What about Beth?'

'She needs me. You don't understand.'

'Or do you need her? You have to go, Joan. You've had your time here.'

The little girl's eyes looked at him with surprise and grief. John seized hold of her and, gently, began to shake. Beth flung her head from side to side, grimacing and panting. He shook harder.

'No, John!' she screamed. 'You're hurting us. No, no, no, no!' At last something faded in her eyes. She seemed to shrink slightly. John wept; he felt as if he had lost his wife all over again. When she was still again, he pulled his daughter next to him into the bed, and waited quietly until she spoke.

'Daddy?'

'Beth?'

'Where's Mummy gone?'

He picked her up and plonked her on his stomach.

'That lady,' he said.

'Was she Mummy?'

'She is someone,' he told her carefully, 'who has no right to be here. Can you keep her away?'

'I think so.'

'Close the door on her, Beth,' he said, although the words caught in his throat. 'Close the door on them all,' he added. To his relief, Beth nodded. She looked as relieved as he felt.

'It's your right,' he told her. 'They're more trouble than they're worth. That lady in particular,' he added, feeling wretched for adding that rider and wondering if, in years still to come, Beth might hold it against him.

After a few more sessions with the hypnotherapist, Beth accomplished what he asked her to do. She shut the door, and shut it so firmly that no one had passed through it for fourteen years. But something else disappeared as well. Beth never mentioned her mother again, and some years later John realised, with a dreadful pang, that she retained no memories of her whatsoever.

Beth listened intently as her father sketched in the details. Different voices. She'd been like a little radio all on her own, he said, trying to make light of it. But he couldn't hide from her how disturbed he had been at the time.

'The therapist was very good. He told you to keep the door shut, and you did.'

The wrong door, thought Beth. The wrong door.

John looked at her and raised his eyebrows. 'I still have the number,' he said. 'I can call him again, if you like.'

666

Charles Peters had put on a lot of weight since the last time he had treated Beth. He'd been stout then; now he was enormous. He was dressed in a huge black suit with a polo-neck shirt tucked firmly into his trousers, held in place by a belt that dug in so deeply it looked painful. He had a high, melodious voice, wore thick-framed black glasses and had his hair tied back in a greying ponytail. He looked every inch like a very fleshy cartoon hypnotist.

All three of them sat together and discussed the problem. Charles suggested hypnotism and visual-isation – the same as before.

'It's a very simple thing,' he told her. 'You'll be conscious the whole time. I'll just ask you to relax a little more deeply than you normally would while you're awake. You probably won't even notice that anything's happening.'

Beth nodded.

'The first thing I want to do is find out if this episode is related to what happened last time.'

Beth felt her dad cast her an anxious glance.

'Back then,' said Charles, 'you were dreaming that you were someone else – in this case, your mother. It's not uncommon. Have you been dreaming of her again at all?' Beth shook her head. 'Right. It may be that what you're experiencing now is a leftover from that time, or it may be something entirely new. Once we find out, we can start to think about what we want to do about it. OK?'

The whole thing wasn't going to take more than half an hour. Charles asked John to sit in the waiting room until they were done and got Beth to move to a more comfortable chair. 'But not too comfortable – I don't want you falling asleep,' he told her. Beth took her place in a wide but firm armchair with a high, straight back, and waited anxiously to see what would happen.

The hypnotherapist told her to close her eyes and relax.

'I want you to imagine', he said, 'that you're walking into a house, a place that you feel comfortable with. A safe, happy place. Can you do that for me?'

Beth thought of the home where she had grown up. She had never felt safer anywhere than there.

'Where are you, Beth?' Charles's voice was soft and reassuring.

'I'm at home. In the hall.'

'Very good. Is that hallway usually carpeted?'

'No, it's boards.'

'Great. Well, I want you to look down, Beth, and as you do that, in those boards right there on the floor, there's a trapdoor. It's a door you always knew was there but, for some reason or other, you forgot all about it. Do you have a cellar in your house?'

'No.'

'Well, now you do. It's kind of mysterious but not in any way dangerous. Just interesting. You bend down . . .' Beth felt her knees flexing involuntarily as she acted out his instructions in her mind '. . . and you pull the door open. In front of you now, Beth, you can see some steps going down into the ground.

A soft, warm light is coming up at you. It's nice. It's inviting. You like the look of it down there.'

The hypnotist's low, slightly monotonous voice droned on. Beth relaxed more deeply. In her mind, she began to walk down into the cellar. It smelt warm.

'It's warm, it's familiar. You're at home. Everything is relaxed, everything is safe.'

In her chair, Beth sighed. He was right – yes, she did feel safe.

'Are you down there, Beth?' Charles asked. He leaned forward in his chair to watch her closely.

'Yes.'

'Look around you. Tell me what you see.'

'There's someone else here,' murmured the entranced girl.

'Oh? And do you know who it is?'

Beth looked up, straight into his eyes. She smiled. '*Grata mundo meo*,' she said – in someone else's voice.

John waited a little over half an hour. At the end of it his daughter walked out and looked blankly at him.

'OK?' he asked.

'Fine.'

He looked over her shoulder into the treatment room.

'Don't go in – he's taking a call,' said Beth.

'Did you make another appointment?'

'He said he'd ring.'

They had a short conversation in the car on the way back, but Beth was vague about what had happened. John didn't question it – she had been hypnotised, after all. At home she said she was tired and went straight up to her room.

John stayed on and drank tea with Louis, but two hours later Beth was still up there. He went to knock softly on her door but there was no answer. He tried the handle. The door was locked. John had clients to meet, and he left reluctantly without seeing any more of her, leaving a message for her to ring when she awoke. Louis called later, to report in. Beth had come down in the evening to eat, watched a little TV, and gone to bed early. She looked relaxed. Louis felt that the hypnosis session had done some good, and promised to call again if there was any news.

John would have liked to have heard from his daughter, and from Peters, come to that. But Beth wasn't his little girl any more and it wasn't up to him to grill her therapist. Louis reassured him, though, and John went to bed hopeful that the problem, if a problem it was, had been nipped in the bud.

666

That night, a Thursday, Louis and Ivan went out for

a drink. Louis went home early but Ivan ended up going on to a house party. He didn't enjoy it much. It was annoying. He could have got a lot less drunk and gone to bed with one of at least three first-year girls he'd met there. But there was no way. If he had it would have got back to Louis – and if it got back to Louis, it would get back to Beth.

The previous year, having alienated the girls in his own year with lechery and lies, Ivan had eyed the new intake limping into his territory with something like glee. He'd looked forward to Freshers this year, too – but for reasons beyond his control it had all gone tits up. Instead of bouncing happily from bed to bed, he got himself hung up on practically the first girl he slept with.

It was such a pain. He'd only discovered sex a few years earlier and he'd been looking forward to at least a decade of happy no-strings-attached lechery. Why Beth? He didn't understand. All he knew was that for the first time in his life he was moping about either waiting for her to call, or plucking up courage to call her. Worst of all, he was turning down other offers in case it put Beth off.

Hopefully, a few more bangs would sort it out and he could get back to normal. The problem was, his reputation preceded him. An easygoing personality, good looks and a willingness to lie through his teeth had served him very well so far, but now these qualities had turned round and bitten him on the arse. Beth had made it very clear when she'd agreed to go to bed with him that she knew all about him – and it was fine! This was just a bit of fun between two consenting adults. OK? Great. And now he was stuffed, because the minute he started trying to tell her how much he was thinking of her the shutters came down. He had said the same thing before, so often, to so many other girls.

Even Ivan had the sense to know that someone stricken with the vomits was unlikely to want too much attention. He'd been leaving her alone, trying to show her how considerate he was. The trouble was – did she realise this? Someone needed to point out to her just how considerate he was being in case she mistook it for a lack of interest. With this thought in mind, he had pinched some flowers he'd found in a vase at the party earlier and was planning to lay them on her bed for her to find in the morning. See? He could do romance. No problem.

He came in at about half-four in the morning, having passed out on a pile of coats in a drunken stupor some hours previously. There was a light on in the bathroom. Someone was in the shower. Odd. He was about halfway up the stairs when the door opened and Beth came out, steaming, beautiful and completely bare. She saw him at once and paused. If he had looked more closely, Ivan might have noticed the bruises beginning to show on her arms, but her arms weren't what he was looking at. Forcing his eyes away from her body, he gave her his sweetest smile and held out the flowers. Beth stepped back into the bathroom and shut the door.

His heart beating with desire, Ivan tiptoed up the remaining steps and stopped outside the bathroom door. 'Sorry,' he whispered. There was no answer. 'You're gorgeous,' he added.

A moment later the door opened and Beth appeared again, this time wearing a dressing gown. Ivan held out the flowers once more. She glanced at him suspiciously before ducking past him and into her room. He paused. He still had his flowers to give her. He tapped lightly on the door. If you don't ask, he thought, you don't get . . .

'Beth.'

Still no answer.

'Beth?'

No answer.

'Go on,' he said. He waited a moment, then added, 'I'm coming in.' He moved the door handle slightly, and when there was no response pushed it down properly and entered.

Beth was standing by the bed, watching him

curiously. She licked her lips. Ivan decided to take this as a good sign.

'Beth,' he said hoarsely. He stepped up to her. She smelled sweet and clean. She didn't move, just stood there with her head tipped slightly to one side, watching him.

He stepped right up to her and put a hand on her waist. He waited for her to put her arms around him but she still didn't respond. He tried to smile. This was killing him. '. . . have another look?' he suggested. Gingerly, he tugged at the belt to her dressing gown. She put her hand on his to stop him, but didn't move away.

'You're beautiful,' Ivan said, and went in for the kill. He kissed her, but apart from tilting her head up slightly she didn't respond. Disconcerting. He caressed her, nuzzled her neck, and lifted a hand to her breast. Encouraged, he reached down, sought out the gap in her gown, and touched her lightly between her legs.

Beth pushed him back, spun him round, and picked him up by the belt and collar. She carried him to the door as if he weighed no more than a biscuit, paused while he obediently opened it for her, and tossed him lightly out of the room.

Ivan fell heavily onto the landing and clutched at the banister to stop himself falling downstairs. He turned in time to see Beth closing the door. She paused to smile sweetly at him and spoke for the first time.

'Anuzzer time,' she said, in what he took for a mock accent. The door closed. Ivan scrambled to his feet, panting with desire.

It was official. Ivan was in love.

Chapter Three

The following morning Beth awoke crippled again. Terrible black bruises had blossomed all over her in the night, on her arms and legs. She could hardly move. She didn't even try to get out of bed this time. She just lay there, too exhausted to even weep.

Louis dropped in and made a fuss about calling a doctor. She hid her bruises under the duvet and refused, claiming to be ill with flu. All she needed was sleep. Then Coll turned up and said the same thing. This time she agreed – tomorrow, if things were no better. But for now – sleep, sleep. Just let me sleep.

They left, and sleep she did – hours and hours of it, unbroken and seamless. She awoke briefly again in the evening and begged for food – pizza and fish and chips.

'Pizza AND fish and chips?' repeated Coll. 'Wow. That's comfort eating off the scale.'

Beth ate the lot and fell back to sleep again at once. She didn't wake up until the following morning; and at last, after three days of it, she was feeling better. She had slept through. Her body was still in pain, every muscle hurt. But it was better, definitely. Perhaps — she dared hope — whatever had possessed her had passed on.

The next day her recovery continued. The bruising in her muscles had lessened. She dozed through the day, and got up and sat with the others in the living room in the evening. There was general relief that she seemed to be getting back to her old self, although she wasn't sure that either Louis or Coll were really convinced. Coll accused her of having Eating Disease. Louis thought she had worms. Ivan offered her a stomach massage. She still kept her gloves on, which everyone obviously thought was weird but did not mention. Under them, her hands too were healing. It was a good night. She had a few drinks and a laugh, and went back to bed feeling anxious but optimistic.

The next day there was a call from her dad. The police had been round. Charles Peters had disappeared.

'I'm coming over,' he said.

'I didn't do anything.'

'No, but —'

'I didn't do anything!'

'I know you didn't. *They* know you didn't too, but they have to question everyone.' He paused. 'You're bound to be upset.'

Beth chewed the leather tip off her glove. 'They'll want to know about the sleepwalking,' she complained.

'Well, they already know, Beth. They asked why you were seeing him and I told them. Apparently you were his last appointment before he disappeared. Look, it's just routine – you're the last person they'll be worrying about. Anyway, I'm on my way round. And Beth, listen. I want you to come home with me.'

'What for?'

'Just for a stay. Let's discuss it when I get there.'

Beth put down the phone. She thought back and realised for the first time that she had no memory whatsoever of the therapist after he had hypnotised her. Her head had been emptied. It was if her own life was happening to another person. The dirt in her bed, the raided grave, the exhaustion, the hunger . . .

Now this.

The police ought to know, surely, that she was going mad? And her dad. She hadn't told him half of it. What about her housemates? What if she turned on them?

But I haven't done anything! she thought. And she pushed these crazy thoughts away, locked them down deep inside her, even though she knew that inside her was exactly where the danger lurked.

John turned up as promised and hung around for a few hours, wanting to help but not knowing how. He had assumed that the police were going to go straight round to Beth, but they didn't show – not yet, anyway.

The fact was, they weren't that bothered. The alert had been given by the therapist's mother in Perth, Australia. He rang her without fail every Wednesday, so how come not this week? The mother, a hawkish woman, had hissed and nagged down the phone, and the investigating officer, Inspector Burrows, considered that Charlie Peters might have been happy not to ring her for once. But he sent one of his officers round to ask a few questions anyway. Peters had left his practice without warning, and with no cover, which was odd. Even so, few disappearances turned out to be serious. The likelihood was that he had gone through some unknown personal crisis and run away. If at some point they did decide to treat the disappearance as suspicious, they had plenty of far more promising lines of inquiry to follow than Beth. Peters had a string of male lovers scattered around the country, as far afield as London and Glasgow. Chances were he was ensconced in some lover's flat, or had run off with a young man from Cardiff he had been seeing lately. There was no hurry to see Beth. They had most of the information they needed from John.

Unable to help in any meaningful way, John nagged at Beth to come home and spend some time with him. But she was having none of it. She'd only just left home. To run back to daddy now, at the first sign of trouble? No way. John pressed her; she grew irritable. He had to back down.

'Look after her,' he told his son, and he was foolish enough to say it in front of Beth. She swore and stormed off. Louis nodded. He would. You bet. He planned to try and talk to her about it that very night, whether she got angry or not. As it happened, though, Beth went out for a drink with Coll and he missed his chance.

There were any number of bars and little eateries up and down the Wilmslow Road, close to where they lived in Fallowfield south Manchester. Beth and Coll settled themselves down in a booth in a little place called Blue, just by the main road, with a big glass of wine each. Coll wasted no time. 'So what's going on, Bethie?'

Beth shook her head. 'Just ill,' she said.

Coll reached across the table and took her hand. Beth pulled away, but not hard. Gently, Coll removed the glove and rolled up her friend's sleeve to reveal the healing skin and a series of deep bruises, all the colours of the rainbow, up her forearm.

'You need to tell me about this.'

Beth took back her arm. She took a swig of wine, looked at Coll's frightened white face and winced. It was all so crazy, so unlikely — so impossible. She was scared of letting the cat out of the bag.

'Does Louis know?' she asked.

Coll shook her head. 'Don't think so.'

'How did you spot it?'

'I crept in while you were asleep and had a peep.' Beth smiled ruefully, and Coll laughed. 'Sorry, doll,' she said. 'But I'm not taking no for an answer. And I'm not going to find out by osmosis, either, am I?'

Beth took a breath. She had been silent too long. Time to take the plunge.

She told her story in parts. First the believable. The exhaustion. Sleepwalking. The hunger. Coll listened very carefully, very seriously, without mocking or scoffing. Encouraged, Beth jumped right in.

The dirt under her nails, the mysterious showering at night. The raided grave . . .

Coll was appalled.

'Bethie! And you've been going through all this on your own? You've been driving me crazy – and Louis. Why didn't you say something?'

'But what if it's true?'

'Of course it's not true! But that doesn't mean it's not serious. Oh, you poor darling . . .'

'But what about the brick? Where did that come from?'

'The world's full of bricks, even Roman ones. There's a whole cathedral made of them in St Alban's. You've been hearing stuff on the radio and then you've been tying it in, that's all. Come on, babe, what do you want me to say – that you've been disinterring bodies you didn't even know existed? Sleepwalking – fine. But sleep *digging*? Let's get real here. That therapist going missing has really screwed with your brain.' Coll shook her head. 'And look at your arms! You *have* been doing something in your sleep, but God knows what. Falling downstairs or something. Jesus, Bethie, you could kill yourself like this. You've got to get this fixed. What's worrying you? Any ideas?'

Beth shook her head. What was that dark place inside that kept threatening to overwhelm her?

Coll thought she'd found a clue when she told that part of the story about her speaking to her dad in her mother's voice.

'Jesus,' she said. 'Freud would have wet his baggy little Austrian Y-fronts to get his hands on you. But it kind of fits. You lost your mother when you were four. You blame yourself for it. Babe, you have some issues to deal with here and your subconscious is doing one hell of a job of hiding it from you.' She took a swing of her drink. 'Fortunately,' she added, 'the stories it's trying to convince you with are such complete shite, you'd have to be four years old to believe them.' Coll shook her head. 'Why does the mind go to all that trouble to hide the real issues from you, and then pick such bollocks to fool you with?'

Beth nodded. Yes. Exactly. Bollocks. That's what it was. Utter shite, once you started to think about it like that.

'Of course,' remarked Coll, 'it does mean you're one crazy girl, Beth. Box of frogs doesn't get near it. You need help. If you're walking about on your own, asleep, anything could happen. Judging by your arms, it already has.'

Beth nodded. It was a sobering thought, but at least it was explicable – if not exactly normal.

'I'm just bonkers, then,' she said.

''Fraid so.' Coll smiled and shrugged. 'But not barking mad. You've just been sitting on stuff that needs dealing with, that's all. It's common as muck. Not stuff you can deal with on your own, though. Your dad had the right idea. You need counselling.'

Being bonkers wasn't exactly good news, but it was so much better than the way things had seemed only a day or so ago that Beth felt positively elated at the prospect. Right, she thought – that was that sorted. Now it was time to enjoy herself. She emptied her glass. 'Let's drink,' she said, getting up to go to the bar.

'That's my girl,' said Coll. 'Hey! Let's do cocktails. Let's get totally rat-arsed!'

So they did. They came home hours later and pulled Beth's room to pieces, examined the doormat, Beth's clothes and anything else they could think of. They found nothing except a few dirty footprints, half smudged away, on the carpet near the bed.

'Grave dirt,' said Coll, snorting with laughter. It was hilarious. They laughed and laughed and laughed. Grave dirt! As if.

Beth was looking up some music online in her room, when her friend came in with a blow-up mattress, sat on the floor and started to inflate it.

'What are you doing?'

'Standing guard. Sleeping guard, I mean. If you

want to go for a walk tonight, it's over my sleeping body.'

Beth watched her puff away.

'Actually,' she said. She got up and went to the door.

'What?' said Coll.

'I'm going to . . .'

'Are you?'

'For one night only.'

'That's what you said last time.'

'I know.' Beth grinned excitedly.

Coll grinned back.

'Who am I to talk?' she said. 'Enjoy! Just . . .'

'What?'

'Make sure you use him before he uses you.'

'Consider it done.'

Beth tiptoed out the door and down the corridor. Ivan, of course, was delighted to see her. 'You said you wouldn't do it with me the other day,' he complained.

Beth slipped into bed beside him and buried her face in his shoulder.

'A reprieve. I had some good news.'

'What's that?' he asked, moving his hand up her back. She shivered deliciously.

'I'm crazy. I wouldn't be here otherwise, would I?'

Ivan laughed, and slid down the bed to kiss her.

'Hey – what's this?' he demanded shortly after. He had found the bruises on her body. 'What happened?'

'I've been sleepwalking. I fell downstairs. Do you mind? You'll have to be gentle.'

Ivan nodded, and was as good as his word.

Chapter Four

The police turned up the next morning when Beth was still in bed with Ivan. Louis called up to her – typically, because that meant he'd find out where she'd slept – and she had to pull on some clothes and hurry down. There was just one female officer. All she needed to do was confirm what John had told them and check to see if Peters had said anything odd during the session.

'Thanks, that's it,' the policewoman said. 'Sorry about the questions. It's what we do.' She smiled. 'Must be a bit weird, having your counsellor disappear on you overnight like that.'

'It was a bit,' Beth admitted. 'Any idea where he is?'

'He probably just took off. People do it all the time. He'll turn up. Your dad said you were seeing him about sleepwalking. Did he manage to sort it out?'

'Actually, yes,' said Beth.

'Maybe he did his job, then,' the officer said. Beth nodded. Maybe he had.

'Don't say a word,' she told Louis when she went into the kitchen to make tea afterwards.

'I didn't.'

'It's a one-off.'

Louis shrugged. 'None of my business,' he said.

'Exactly.' Beth got on with making tea. 'But I can feel you disapproving of me,' she told him. It was exasperating, but in her good mood she couldn't help laughing at him.

Louis grinned back. 'Ivan's my mate,' he said. 'But you're my sister.'

Beth wasn't going to argue. She was determined not to let Louis burst her bubble. 'Look, I know you're just thinking about me,' she said. 'But it's my decision, right?'

'Absolutely. I've been more worried about how you are. You've been really weird.'

'I've been ill! What do you expect?'

'OK.' Her brother raised his hands in surrender. He got up. 'We were supposed to be playing football this morning. I guess this means he's not going to make it.'

'No – I'm going up. I'll tell him.'

Upstairs, Beth drank her tea sitting on the side of the bed and resisted Ivan's invitation to get back in. He had made her feel so much better about herself, she was almost tempted to believe him when he said he wanted her and her alone. Maybe he was actually being sincere; who knew? She was inclined to think he was, but she wasn't willing – yet – to risk it.

Ivan went off to play football, and Beth went back for another luxurious few hours in bed. She had a few things to sort out that day, including ringing her dad to ask him to sort out another counsellor for her. Coll collared her and told her to let Louis in on what was really happening. He was her brother, he loved her, he deserved to know – and he would sleep lightly for her at night in case she got up and walked again.

'And tell Ivan, too,' said Coll. 'If we all know, we stand a better chance of catching you at it and stopping you.'

Beth nodded. Absolutely. Of course. It was a good idea. But at the back of her mind was the hope that the whole thing had stopped as mysteriously as it had started. By the time the evening came round, she'd managed to tell no one at all.

It was a wet December evening, the sort of night for

stopping in with a film on TV. But it was also Friday, just a couple of weekends before uni broke up for Christmas. Soon many of their new friends would be going home for the holiday. There was already a sense of celebration in the air. So instead, they headed out for a drink. The wind blew them up and down the bars on the Wilmslow Road, where they drank and talked, and talked and drank, got separated, met up again, talked some more, drank some more, had a good time. At about eleven p.m. Coll, encouraged by Beth, propositioned Louis, and he turned her down.

'Why?' she demanded. 'Why? Look at me,' she said, spreading her arms to show herself off. 'What is wrong with your brother, Beth?'

'He just has good taste,' yelled Ivan above the music.

Louis shook his head and shrugged. 'Too close to home,' he said. Beth looked significantly at Ivan.

'You mean if I was living somewhere else you'd have sex with me?' demanded Coll. 'Should I give my notice in? Beth? Should I give my notice in?'

Louis groaned and covered his face.

'He's a Christian. He has to be in love first,' explained Beth.

'And you sleep around all over the place,' Ivan pointed out to Coll. 'That makes you an unsuitable Christian bride.'

'I don't want to be his bride. I want to shag him.'

'Please stop,' begged Louis.

'Is it because you're a virgin?' teased Beth. 'All that time with Sam, you were just holding hands and stuff. Is that it?'

'OK, I'm a virgin. Now leave me alone.'

'I'm a virgin too,' said Coll.

'Really?'

'No, but I could try for you.'

'Christ, I dread to think what sort of virginity it is that you haven't lost yet,' groaned Ivan.

'Why me?' demanded Louis. 'Look.' He gestured around the bar. It was full of boys. 'All these. What's special about me?'

'It's a challenge. Like conquering Everest,' said Coll. But she grimaced slightly at Beth, who knew the truth. Coll had adored him ever since the age of eleven.

The upshot of it was that Coll got off with someone else – one of her regulars, she said. She worried about leaving Beth, but Beth swore that she'd already told Louis about the sleepwalking.

'Just go and enjoy yourself,' she said. Later, walking back home, Ivan tried to hold her hand, but she put him off.

'Not back to this again,' he begged.

Beth shook her head. If she slept with him again, they would be going out together. She wasn't ready for that.

'I haven't been with anyone else since the first time, you know,' he told her.

Surely he was lying; but her heart gave a little leap. 'That's not the point. Too close to home,' she said.

'What is it with you guys and this too-close-to-home stuff?' complained Ivan grumpily. He'd fallen in love. Wasn't she supposed to fall in love back? Weren't they supposed to be irresistible to each other? Wasn't she at least supposed to believe whatever he told her?

'It'd be too complicated. Now leave off. Not tonight.'

By the time they got back home, Beth was exhausted again. Her head was beginning to throb. She headed upstairs. Ivan stood at the bottom of the stairs and made puppy-dog eyes at her.

'No,' she said firmly, and went into her room. Ah, she thought, but what if he was tamed by love? What if his heart could be truly hers? What if he was still being faithful in, say, a month? No! Too long, he might get bored. Two weeks? One?

Beth laughed at herself. 'You idiot,' she said.

Her phone pinged a text to her. It was Coll.

'Tell Ivan too,' it said.

Oh. About the sleepwalking. Leaving the house. Yeah. She needed to tell everyone. Then she rolled herself up in her duvet and fell straight to sleep.

Ivan would have liked to stay up and have more beers, but Louis was tired and went to bed soon after Beth. Unlike her, though, he was unable to sleep. His sister scared him – she always had. It was as if a part of his mind was forever hissing at him – 'Watch her! Watch her!'

Tonight it was worse than ever. Something was going on. He knew about the counselling, of course, and his dad had told him about the sleepwalking. He'd meant to talk to her about it but hadn't managed to, mainly because every time he even asked her how she was she almost bit his head off. He'd tried to collar Coll, but she'd told him that it was up to Beth to tell him. It was unfair. Just because he was the one who loved her most, he was the one kept most in the dark.

His head was buzzing. Beth! Beth! Beth! Beth! Every time he fell asleep he woke up with a jerk. Why on Earth was his little sister plaguing him, when neither of them wanted it?

After half an hour of tossing and turning he got up and went downstairs to make a cup of tea, painfully aware that this was what his dad did whenever he couldn't sleep. He sat down at the kitchen table and sniffed the hot steam rising out of his cup. Damn it. He was like some sort of caricature of himself and he wasn't even out of university yet.

There was a creak on the stairs above him.

Louis paused with the tea halfway to his mouth. Another creak – a secretive, careful creak. Ivan on his way to Beth's room? Or . . .

Cautiously he got up from the table, went out into the hallway and peered up the stairs. Beth was standing stock-still a few steps down, fully dressed, wearing her big coat, looking straight ahead. Her face was curiously expressionless.

'Beth?' he called softly.

She didn't answer, or look directly at him, or move in any way. Louis waited a moment and then began to creep up the stairs towards her.

'Beth?' he called again. Her head moved, a little jerk. She seemed to look at him, just a glance, out of the sides of her eyes. Then she turned and made her way back up the stairs and into her bedroom.

It was worse than their father had feared. She'd been about to leave the house in her sleep. He waited a moment more before following her up. He found her lying in bed, fully clothed and shoed, apparently fast asleep.

Louis shook his head. Anything could happen to her! She needed watching.

There was a chair by the table that she did her work on. He got a blanket from his room, wrapped himself up in it, put the chair with its back firmly against the door so that he would have to be moved for her to open it, and sat himself down. He would keep watch over her tonight. Tomorrow he would try to convince her that their dad was right – she needed to go home for a while, until these episodes passed.

Louis settled back in the chair and fixed his gaze on the bed. Beth was lying on her back, her eyes firmly shut. He closed his own eyes for a moment, and when he opened them again her head was raised and her eyes were wide open, staring at him.

'Beth?' he croaked. 'You awake?'

'You're asleep,' she told him. And then he was.

Next door, Ivan too was wide awake, but had failed to hear anything due to having his earplugs in. He'd watched part of a film on his laptop and drunk more beer, but he still wasn't feeling tired. He half-thought about going out – the clubs and bars along the Wilmslow Road would be open for hours yet and there was fun to be had. On the other hand there was

Beth, sleeping next door . . . dreaming, no doubt, of him.

He had most of half a bottle of vodka under his bed and some old orange juice that was still drinkable, more or less. Why not? He'd sneak across and put it to Beth. What better time was there to have some naughties than up here, on a windy night, with her bruv fast asleep next door? It just added to the fun. Maybe she'd let him in. Maybe they'd have a bit of a fumble, or even just a kiss with her hot in her bed. Beth liked a bit of fun. At the very least, she'd think it was a laugh.

Ivan slipped the covers back and stepped out of bed. He pulled on his jeans — he didn't want to give her that much of a fright — and crept out onto the landing. He paused, collecting his thoughts, getting his courage up. Was this wise? She wasn't well. What if he startled her and she screamed? What if she was offended?

He could be in the shit about this — but you know what? Shit and him, they were old friends. He stepped to Beth's door. It was ajar. He eased it open and peered inside, to see a most extraordinary sight.

Beth was standing upright in the middle of the room, fully dressed, with her coat on. Louis was there with her, sitting in a chair, and she was holding the chair up by the seat in the air at chest level with one hand, as if she were about to serve sandwiches on a plate. Louis was the sandwich.

Ivan stared blankly at her. What was it? Some sort of magic trick? No one was that strong. Beth closed her eyes and sighed in an exasperated way. Louis, slouching in the chair, appeared to be fast asleep.

Ivan raised his hands up like a cartoon version of someone on tiptoe and walked backwards out of the room. Clearly what he was seeing wasn't really happening. He carried on down the landing and into his own room. Only when he had pushed the door closed did he hear himself squeaking – literally squeaking like a mouse in fright. He dived into bed and pulled the covers over his head. His heart was going like a road drill. He waited, quaking under the duvet, for nearly a minute, before picking up the courage to peek out to make sure he hadn't been followed . . .

Nothing. Thank God! His head sank back onto the pillow and he groaned silently to himself. What on Earth *was* that? Why was he practically crapping his pants? If this was love, how come it felt just the same as terror? And what was she doing anyway – some sort of circus strongman act? She'd been holding Louis and that chair in the air as if he weighed nothing.

What kind of girl was it he'd fallen for?

There was a sound on the landing. Feet on the floor. Someone stepping . . . stepping, Ivan realised, towards him.

He lay in bed, clutching at the duvet and staring at the door. He reminded himself of a tiny little boy, waiting for a monster to call. Nearer . . . nearer. The door handle slowly turning. Oh Christ.

Louis came in.

'Shit! Louis! You bastard! Christ,' groaned Ivan.

Louis didn't say anything. It occurred to Ivan that he was after him for sneaking into Beth's room.

'I was asleep. I was going to the toilet, I opened the wrong door,' he lied, more or less at random.

'What?'

Ivan opened his mouth to have another go, but there was a creak next door. Louis put his fingers to his lips.

'What was going on in there?' demanded Ivan. 'Why was she carrying you around the bedroom on a chair, Louis? I mean – is it just crazy or is it sick? I can't make up my mind.'

'What are you talking about?' asked Louis.

'Didn't you *see* me? What was it? Are you guys rehearsing for some sort of party trick?'

'Shshssh!' Footsteps next door. A door opened. A creak. Beth was making her way downstairs.

Louis went to the door and listened. 'Was she awake?' he asked.

'What?'

'Beth. Was she awake?'

'You should know, man, she was carrying you around the bedroom in a chair. I mean, where did she get muscles like that? She just looks like a girl, but underneath – man!'

'What do you mean, carrying me around on a chair?'

'What do you think I mean? I mean she was carrying you around the bedroom on a chair.'

Louis stared at him. 'That's ridiculous,' he said.

'Didn't you notice?' demanded Ivan. The whole thing was getting weirder and weirder. He could feel his brain going.

'I was asleep. I just woke up,' said Louis. 'But my chair had moved,' he recalled. 'She was carrying me?' he asked. He had no memory of it at all. He remembered sitting down, and then – blank. He must have fallen asleep.

Downstairs, the front door opened. Louis ran to the window and peered out. Beth, ghostly in the lamplight, was just leaving the front garden. 'She's off,' he said. 'Shit. Ivan, go! We'll lose her.'

'What?'

'You're dressed. I'll get some clothes on and follow

you.' Nothing was going to make Louis go out in the night in his dressing gown. 'Go on! We'll lose her,' he said again.

Ivan went to the window and watched Beth move up the road. 'Right,' he said. He paused. 'What do I do when I catch up with her? Do I wake her up? Isn't it supposed to be dangerous or something?'

Louis paused. He'd heard that about sleepwalkers, too, but wasn't it bullshit – one of those myths? But Beth was disappearing down the road and he didn't have time to think it through. Afterwards, he cursed himself for the decision he arrived at. Play it safe, he thought.

'Just follow her – I'll be there in a minute. Take your phone,' he added. He ran next door to his room to get dressed. Ivan slipped on his trainers and anorak and ran swiftly up the road in the direction he had last seen Beth heading. A figure was walking left down a side street. He slid quietly across the road for a better look. It was her, all right.

He texted Louis: 'Got her.' He waited until she was a way off before he turned the corner and, sticking to the shadows, crept along the pavement after her.

By the time Louis was ready to leave the house there were two texts from Ivan.

'Got her' and 'Left at the main road.'

Louis set off in pursuit through the windy night. He got three more texts before he caught up with Ivan outside a run-down building in a short row of derelict houses and shops, boarded up and waiting for demolition.

'Where is she?'

'In there.' Ivan indicated a dark alley beside one of the dilapidated houses.

'She's down there? Then why are you out here?'

'She can't get out – I checked.'

'Jesus, Ivan, you were supposed to keep an eye on her!'

Louis edged down the passage, with Ivan behind him. It led to a small yard filled with builders' rubble, broken furniture and other rubbish. The only door was boarded with perforated zinc, as were all the ground-floor windows.

The yard was empty.

'You idiot – Ivan, you lost her. She must have climbed out over this somehow,' hissed Louis, look-ing up at the debris heaped against the back wall.

'I'd have heard her,' insisted Ivan, looking anxiously around. He'd been scared to wait in the alley, but the thought that he might have let her down was horrible. That would ruin his chances for good. 'Look – what's that?' He pointed to an unboarded window some ten feet off the ground. A drainpipe led up to it. 'Do you think she went up there?' he asked doubtfully.

'In her sleep?' asked Louis incredulously.

They both stood still for a moment.

'Call her,' said Ivan.

Louis called out gently: 'Beth!'

Ivan snorted in derision. She'd never hear that.

'BETH? You there?' he bellowed.

'Shhhh!' hissed Louis.

Ivan shrugged. They waited in the dark. There was no answer.

'She must have sneaked out. What'll we do?' Ivan began to panic. 'We should have woken her! How come you made me not wake her?'

'All you had to do was keep her in sight.' Louis chewed his lip. 'OK. I'm going to have a look in the house. You try to sneak round the back, see if she got out that way.'

Ivan pulled a face.

'Unless you want to go up there?'

'OK.' Ivan faced the heap of rubbish and put his foot on it gingerly, while Louis grabbed hold of the drainpipe and heaved down on it. It groaned against the wall, but held. Every nerve in his body was screaming at him that this was a very, very bad idea.

Chapter Five

The pipe swung and tugged at its fixings. Louis pulled his way up to the first-floor window where he paused, his head level with the sill. He listened to the house breathing in the wind, creaking, rustling and groaning in the darkness. Mice and rats? The sound of decay? Was it just the wind, rolling and buffeting its way around the city, pushing in through the shutters and cracks?

Or was someone inside?

He called softly: 'Beth?' In the street a car went past. He tried again, a little louder.

'Beth?'

No answer. Louis could never remember being so scared. He groaned and bent his head. In the window-sill he could see marks where someone's fingers had crushed deep into the wood. He touched the sill and pressed down himself, but was unable to make anything like the same impression.

He remembered what Ivan had said. *'She was carrying you around on a chair.'* For the first time, he began to seriously wonder if there was something here that couldn't be understood. As a Christian he was used to that idea, but normally such things stayed firmly on the other side of prayer.

But was this the work of God? Or was it . . . the Other One? Superstitiously, Louis was reluctant to form the word even in thought.

He pushed the fear down, hauled himself up to the window, grunting, and climbed inside. He tried a prayer while his eyes adjusted to the dark.

'Jesus, help and protect me. Bless my sister Beth. In Your name. Amen.'

Jesus didn't answer. He never did. That didn't mean to say He wasn't there in the darkness, right by his side. Yeah? You there, Jesus? You and who else?

Louis stepped forward into the darkness.

The place was a mess. Tramps and kids had got in, but even that was long ago. Now the whole place was just rotten. The roof was going. At some point the builders had tried to keep out the rain with sheets of polythene, but it had got in anyway and run down through all four floors, pulling the plaster off the walls and rotting the boards underfoot. The place was a death trap.

And it stank, he realised. He sniffed – and gagged. It was far worse than just damp. Something had died. A mouse? But it was a big stink. A rat, perhaps. Or a cat? Louis wrinkled his nose and tried to breathe through his mouth.

This is ridiculous, he thought. Creeping about at three in the morning in a deserted house that smelled of death. But if his sister was in here, sleepwalking, she was in danger. The floor could just fall away beneath her. She could die.

So could he.

Louis crept towards the door, stepping over the broken furniture and clumps of fallen plaster. Then, above him, a noise. It was clear this time. Someone was moving about upstairs.

'Beth?' His voice shocked the damp air. Still no answer. But it had to be her. There was no way into the house from downstairs. The only way was up the pipe – no tramp would bother doing that, surely. Louis so much wanted to be somewhere else – in bed preferably – but he made his way towards the stairway and peered up. Some street light was getting in through the broken windows, but it was still very dark.

'Beth!' he hissed desperately. Nothing. He plucked up his courage and tried again, this time really loud.

'Beth!' he yelled. His voice sprang up like a huge bird in the darkness. Upstairs, someone stumbled. But there was still no answer. Louis began to climb the stairs, up to whatever crazy and dismal dream had brought his sister to this place. He put his weight down carefully on each step, for fear of the wood collapsing under him – and with each step the smell of rotting meat increased. He pulled his scarf over his face. The stench was choking. As he got to the top of the stairs he saw someone move rapidly along the corridor and duck out of view.

A human form.

'Beth! Beth, it's me, it's Louis!'

It had to be Beth! It looked like Beth – at least, he thought it did. But she was moving strangely. A moment later he heard noises, above him again. Whoever it was, they were climbing the stairs up to the next floor.

'Beth, bloody hell! Is that you? If it's not Beth, just tell me so I can go away,' he hissed, too scared to yell again. He had started to tremble. Only silence replied. He followed along the corridor and slowly, carefully, climbed the next flight of decaying stairs. The stink of rotting flesh increased tenfold. Whatever it was that had died – a dog, a cat, maybe even a tramp – was surely close by.

He crept as softly as he could along the landing.

Half the plaster had fallen off, leaving the laths like skeleton ribs on the walls and ceiling. The first and second floors had been storage space for the shop that had once occupied the ground floor but it looked as if someone had actually lived up here, long ago. Through the door to one of the bedrooms he could see the remains of a bed, dimly lit by the street lamps outside. It was dark in there — it *was* a bed, wasn't it? It looked as if someone had dragged the mattress off and dumped it to one side.

Louis stared, waiting for his eyes to adjust to the gloom. A great bulk was lying on the mattress, covered with a blanket.

The house sighed around him. Feeling as if he was moving into a dream, Louis walked into the room. The smell increased horrifically. The dead thing must be here, surely, under the blanket on the mattress. He retched on the thick air. Run! Run! Turn around! screamed a voice in his head. But he leaned down and pulled the blanket up and to one side. Even then, when he could see it and know it for what it was, his mind refused to accept. He could feel his eyes fighting to make another sense of it.

It was a man, a hugely fat man, lying on his side. His jacket was open and his black polo shirt was pulled up over his belly. His lips and nose and some of his cheeks were gone, and a large part of his stomach was missing. But that was not even half the horror. There was something else there, curled up inside the corpse, nestling into the body cavity. Something – someone – had made a nest inside the big man; he was pregnant with it. The flesh of this other creature was withered and mummified, its teeth bared in a death's-head grin held together with leathery skin. It had been dead for a very long time – and yet it had eyes – yes, eyes. Louis could see the whites shining palely as it looked up at him.

The withered hands moved. It was alive! Louis jumped back. Something must have knocked against it, surely. But then the leathery jaws opened, a voice croaked something at him, the eyes focused on his, and it tried to sit up.

Louis screamed and fell backwards. As he fell, he was attacked. Arms wrapped around his neck, hauled him upwards onto his feet and started to twist his head sideways. He was in no doubt they intended to turn it the full circle. He grabbed hold of them and tried to pull them off – small hands, he noted, but their strength was out of all proportion to their size.

Louis dropped suddenly to his knees jerking his head free. He swung round and grabbed hold of his attacker's legs. Years of playing rugby had made him strong, but his assailant merely stooped, seized his arms, lifted him up by them and threw him across the room with the force of a machine. He hit the floor and skidded into the wall opposite. He tried to stand up, but he was half-stunned and his attacker was already coming for him again. And at the same time, on the mattress, the creature he had seen nesting in the rotting interior of the fat man's corpse was pulling itself out of the body cavity and turning towards him.

Louis scuttled like a crab across the room. He found a chair and shoved it in front of his attacker but they just knocked it out of the way as if their arms were made of iron. It was too dark to see clearly, but his assailant was clearly human. As they crossed before a window he saw their shape. It was enough to know. It was Beth who was trying to kill him.

He cried out her name. She didn't so much as pause but let out an odd little noise, as if she was clenching her jaws together. Two more steps and she was on him. He tried to fend her off – gently because this was his little sister and he was bigger than she was. But she batted him easily away and, seizing him by the neck, began to squeeze. Louis fell to his knees, choking. He tried to force his thumbs under her grip.

'Beth,' he croaked; and the hands on his neck began to tremble. Their grip faltered. 'Beth, stop. It's me, it's

Louis, please, Beth,' he begged. Another car passed, lighting up her face.

She was crying.

'Please, Beth,' he whispered.

Her eyes had turned dark. It looked as if the whites had been eclipsed. As he spoke her name again, she began to shake violently. Louis seized his chance and pushed her backwards; mistake. She fell back but leaped up into the air instantly without any apparent use of her limbs, landing on all fours. She turned to face him and let out a strange, hooting, high-pitched laugh, the unearthly cry of some kind of animal he had once heard. Then she jumped at him like a dog. She seized his arm in her jaws and his face in her hands, and bit down. Her teeth sheared right through his coat and into his arm.

Louis screamed and tried to release himself. There was a noise behind him. Above the half-devoured belly of the fat man, the shrivelled head of the living corpse, the nest-builder, peered at him, its lidless eyes staring as it rose slowly to its feet.

'Please, Jesus, help me,' gasped Louis. The creature made a rasping, harsh noise that he thought might be a laugh.

'*Fer eum ad me — statim fer eum ad me*,' it spat.

Beth began to drag Louis with her teeth towards the nightmare. He seized hold of her head, wanting to beat at her, but he was still unable to strike his sister. He began to shake and scream and beg: 'No, Beth, no, no, not there, not that, not there . . . please, Beth, no!'

'Louis! What's going on?'

Ivan – downstairs, still outside . . .

'Help, help, Ivan, help, help!' Louis screamed. Below he could hear his friend scramble up the pipe. Beth heard it too. She growled like a dog, and heaved more strongly than ever at Louis, dragging and pushing him into the corner where the creature, the half-dead, half-living thing, was waiting for him. It leaned forward. Its jaws opened and it spoke again.

'*Noli me relinquere, Beth, dilectione mea . . . Oportet nos occidere puerum istum si simul maneamus. Adiuva me, adiuva me, adiuva me.*'

Then, to his horror, it dropped down onto all fours and began to creep across the floor towards them.

'Beth!' Louis cried. He felt her tremble again and through his terror he remembered that she had responded to her name. 'Beth, Beth, it's Louis, it's Louis, Beth, it's Louis,' he began to chant.

Again, the pause. This time Louis didn't try to force her away or fight her. He reached out with his hand and touched her face.

'Beth,' he whispered, trying to stay calm. 'Beth, come back. Come back to me, Beth. It's Louis.'

She turned at last to face him. Her eyes had rolled right up into her head: all he could see were the whites, which had turned a dirty brown. She began to shake again. Louis looked across. The creature, on its hands and knees, was already halfway towards him.

There was a stampede on the stairs – Ivan, on his way up. He burst into the room but paused, brought short by the stink of death in the darkness.

'What the fuck?' he yelled.

'Wait!' shouted Louis. He turned his attention back to his sister. 'Beth,' he begged. 'Come back, Beth. Beth, we have to get out of here now.'

All the time he was speaking, the corpse-creature was crawling towards them. Now it reached a hand out to them. It took all Louis's willpower not to run.

'Beth . . .'

Beth's eyes rolled down in her head and turned sideways, as if she could see behind her to where the creature was. Her face spasmed, and for the first time she managed to speak in her own voice through clenched teeth. 'It's fucking real . . . it's fucking real. Louis . . . help me . . .' she croaked.

'Let's go,' said Louis. He stood up. The living corpse was just a metre away. Beth's eyes rolled in her head again.

'Take her and go,' she croaked, in another voice, not hers.

'What is going on here?' demanded Ivan.

'Her. Me!' shouted Beth suddenly, in two voices but with the same breath.

'Let's go!' yelled Louis. He grabbed her arm and broke for the door, but she still resisted. Another car went past and lit up the room. For the first time, Ivan saw what they were up against. He screamed in terror.

The thing stretched an arm out to Beth. '*Succurre mei, Beth,*' it crooned. '*Nutrere me, nutrere . . .*'

Beth backed away, but her movements were sluggish. With a convulsive movement, the thing lurched to its feet, lunged forward and grabbed her by the leg. Suddenly she was a dead weight, standing there. Louis pushed the corpse; it staggered but held firm and began to claw its way up Beth's legs. He shoved again, but it hardly moved. Its strength seemed to be increasing as he watched. It began to smile. Then there was a flicker in its eyes. Louis began to look back over his shoulder, but even as he moved a beam of timber hurtled past him like a missile and struck the creature straight in the face. The thing fell away backwards without a sound – how could it, with a face full of wood?

Ivan's eyes had adjusted to the dark. 'You stinking little bastard,' he screamed. Over and over again, he rammed the beam down onto the thing's head and face. Whatever it was, he was pounding it to paste.

Louis dragged Beth along the corridor. His foot stabbed through the rotten boards. He wrenched it free and ran on down the stairs, pulling his sister behind him. Above them Ivan was still at work.

'Ivan! Run!' Louis yelled. There was a pause, while Ivan realised he was on his own. Then came the stampede as he came chasing after them. By the time Louis was at the second set of stairs Ivan was pushing past them. There were a terrible few minutes at the final window when they were all struggling out down the pipe, expecting the monster to appear behind them at any moment. Then, suddenly, they were rolling on their backs in the yard in the clean air.

The wind had turned cold and it was trying to rain – a normal Manchester night. But the world had changed. They ran home, glancing behind them. Louis held on to his sister's arm and kept repeating her name . . .

'Beth . . . Beth, you OK? I'm with you, Beth . . . Beth?' He made her look at him and nod. He kept it up until he felt foolish and stopped, but she begged him to keep speaking her name all the way. They were halfway back when Ivan stopped and grabbed hold of Louis by his coat. 'What the fuck was *that*?' he begged. 'What have I done? I killed someone, didn't I?'

'It wasn't a person,' said Beth.

'Then what was it?'

'I don't know.'

They stopped on the street and looked at each other. What had they met? What had they done?

'I must have dug it up out of that grave,' said Beth.

'Fuck this,' said Ivan. 'I didn't ask to get stuck in no horror film.'

'It's over now,' said Louis.

'No,' said Beth. 'It's just begun.' She paused. 'Is it dead?' she asked. 'We ought to go back and see.'

'Are you crazy?' yelled Ivan.

'We are going home,' said Louis. 'I mean right now.' Beth stood still on the street, undecided, until he took her by the arm and led her away. Then suddenly the fear and the hunger came again and she turned and ran.

Chapter Six

Life is an ordinary thing. It's knowable. What lies beyond we can only guess at from the shadows death casts. Look at this in the darkness. Does it have a face? Could it be . . . is it possible . . . do you think?

All that had changed. Now they knew that demons crawl up from hell, that the dead sit under the bed at night, waiting for you to step out. The creatures of shadow and night exist. It is reasonable to be scared of the dark, to jump at unexpected noises and to shiver in your bed when something creaks beneath the boards. Death was out of the box. Nothing could be taken for granted ever again.

They'd seen it. Worse, it had seen them.

In her sleep at night Beth had raided the grave in the local churchyard and released this horror into the world. The enormous half-eaten corpse in the derelict house was the remains of Charles Peters, the hypnotherapist. Somehow, she must have murdered him and dragged his twenty-five-stone body halfway across Manchester, unseen, to the ruined shop. The finger marks that Louis had spotted sunk deep in the wood of the windowsill were hers; they told of the power she'd possessed that night as she'd dragged the body up through the window. That strength was not hers.

Louis did not believe that the drainpipe he had climbed could have taken such a weight. In which case, how had she got the corpse up there? Had she jumped?

It wasn't possible. At least, it hadn't been until now.

At last Beth understood the darkness that had flowered inside her, the raging hunger that had come from nowhere. The darkness was the darkness of the grave; the hunger, the hunger of the dead for life. But how had it reached out for her? Was she possessed, or under some kind of spell? She told the others about the brick and the inscription on it that she had mysteriously been able to translate, despite knowing no Latin at all: 'the Hunger that never ends'. It had to be something to do with that. Should they destroy it? Exorcise it? Or should they just throw it away?

An argument broke out between Louis and Ivan. Ivan wanted to take it outside and pound it to dust with the biggest hammer he could find. Louis thought they should take it back to the churchyard it had come from. It had spent hundreds of years lying there in the ground, doing no harm. Why not just put it back?

'It's what was buried with it that worries me,' said Beth. But the brick itself worried her. She was certain that the creature from the grave feared it even more than she did. Somehow, it was a key to solving the mystery. She refused to let it go until they knew what part it played.

Beth had been possessed by the grave creature itself. But what on earth was it?

'It was one nasty motherfucker, that's all I know,' said Ivan.

'It's dead now,' Louis said.

'Maybe,' said Beth. But she wasn't convinced.

'A demon?' suggested Louis. He had seen pure evil in that room last night. Nothing else fitted. This was an enemy of life – an enemy of God Himself.

'You said it was living inside the corpse,' said Ivan. 'Doesn't that make it a ghoul?'

'But it killed its prey. Ghouls eat carrion, don't they?'

The boys began to squabble about whether they

had discovered a demon or a ghoul, but Beth was only half-listening. No matter which way she thought about this thing, she was arriving at the same conclusion. 'Listen. You know what?' she said, 'It's bad news, but there's no way out of it. We do actually have to go back.'

'What for?' demanded Louis.

'To see if there's a body there. To find out if it stays dead.'

Ivan was furious. 'You do not go back in the haunted house,' he raged.

'Even if the haunted house can come to you?'

'Even if it can catch the bus. No way.'

'But she's right,' said Louis. 'We need to make sure.'

Ivan groaned. Beth gave him a crooked smile. 'Vote on it?' she said.

'I'm in a majority of one on this,' he replied.

'What about Beth?' Louis demanded. '*We* may be able to run away, but she can't, can she?'

But Ivan wasn't having it. 'It's crazy,' he insisted. 'You saw that thing. It's mad to go back.' But he couldn't meet Beth's gaze.

'Just you and me, then, sis,' Louis said, looking grimly at him.

'Yeah.' Beth looked at Louis sitting there, angry with Ivan on her behalf, and she realised . . . 'You're ridiculously faithful, you know that, Louis?' She leaned over and patted him. 'I've been such a bitch and you never even flickered. Even now. It doesn't even occur to you to leave me to it, does it?'

Louis rolled his eyes. It was true, he hadn't even thought about it. He was surprised himself.

Another row broke out. Beth wanted to let Ivan off the hook – what business was this of his? But Louis wasn't having it. They had a duty, he believed. No one else was going to believe what had happened. They had to sort it out, not just for Beth's sake – for the sake of everyone else as well.

The argument went to and fro. Ivan stormed out at one point, furious that Louis had accused him of cowardice. It was madness – it was duty. It was suicide – it was all for Beth. In the end though, Ivan was unable to abandon her.

'I'll come – on one condition,' he said. 'We go armed. And I'm not talking about sharpened pencils here. I'm talking about the works. I want some major anti-demon weaponry. I want guns, I want silver bullets. I want garlic, I want holy water. I want stuff that works.'

'That's it!' Beth was delighted. That was better! Something practical. They could fight back.

'How do we know what works and what doesn't work?' Louis wanted to know.

'We need to read up,' said Beth.

Ivan pulled a face. 'Research,' he groaned. 'I wouldn't even know where to start.'

'Neither would I,' said Beth. 'But I know someone who will.'

Coll had never been the brightest star in the sky when it came to human behaviour. But when she got back home later that day and Ivan asked her if she'd done any more research into Beth's brick she was immediately on the alert.

'Since when were you interested in brick research?' she asked.

'Just curious,' said Ivan.

They were drinking tea round the table. Not only Ivan, but Louis and Beth as well were watching Coll closely. 'What's going on?' she demanded, putting down her mug.

'We were just talking about it,' said Beth.

Coll looked at her doubtfully. 'Well, I found out the rest of that quote for one thing,' she said. 'It's from an old Roman tomb excavated in Syria in the early seventeenth century. "For the living, life. For the dead, the hunger that never ends." Remember?'

'Oh, shit,' said Ivan.

'What about it? Do you know what it means?' demanded Coll.

'We're getting there,' muttered Ivan.

'So what was buried in this tomb?' asked Louis.

'Why? What's it to you?' No one answered. Coll was getting annoyed. She hated being kept in the dark. 'No one's sure. It was raided shortly after it was discovered.'

'Seventeenth century,' said Louis. 'It was round about then that the St Michael's grave must have been dug.'

'OK. What's going on?' said Coll. 'Don't play games with me. You all look like spies at an international spying conference. What's the big secret?'

Beth hesitated. They had been unsure about whether to tell Coll exactly what was going on. It was unfair to put someone else in danger. But they needed all the help they could get, and Coll was bound to be a real asset.

'We reckon that brick came from the robbed grave at St Michael's.'

'You're kidding me,' said Coll. She thought about it. 'But . . .' She turned to look at Beth. 'If that brick came out of the grave, how did you get hold of it?'

'I'm going to tell her,' said Ivan. 'She almost knows already.'

'No, you're not,' Louis insisted.

But Ivan did anyway. Actually, they had little

choice. There was no way Coll was going to let this go. This was a girl who'd stopped believing in Father Christmas at the age of four on the grounds that, if he was supposed to give out gifts according to how good you were, how come it was always the rich kids who were gooder than everyone else? When they weren't? Everyone knew that Brian Winterfold, for example, was both rich and bad, and he got everything he asked for and more, whereas Coll had been as good as gold. So where was the bike?

'You idiots,' she told her housemates. According to them, whatever had been buried in some Roman tomb two thousand years ago had been dug up in the seventeenth century and reinterred in the grave at St Michael's, where Beth in turn had dug it up just a few nights ago. Now, apparently, it was on the loose, getting Beth to kill people so that it could eat them. And why? Because Coll's best friend had been supernaturally enslaved – by a brick. Coll could hardly believe anyone could be so stupid.

'We don't *know* that stuff about the brick,' said Louis weakly. 'That's just a theory. She might be possessed.'

'There isn't any "theory" about it,' Coll told him. 'Corpses do not come back to life. Not even fresh ones, let alone ones that have been dead for four hundred years. You're not even a corpse any more after that long. You two really are a pair of utter fuckwits,' she told Louis and Ivan. 'Poor Bethie here has really been going through it, sleepwalking and dead mothers and stuff, and here you are telling her that her nightmares are real. Louis, I'm seriously unimpressed.'

'You're so sure of yourself,' Ivan said irritably. 'Maybe you know less than you think you do.'

'I'm quite prepared to believe there are things we know nothing about,' Coll said.

'Big of you.'

'It's just that none of them happen to involve dead people coming back to life. You're dead, period. That's it. You get dead, you stay dead.'

'That's what I thought until last night,' said Ivan.

Louis sighed. 'You know what, Coll – I'm really hoping you can come up with a better explanation. I'd be so happy to believe it.'

Coll considered. It would take a whole truckload of psychiatrists to unravel this mess but she reckoned she could make a pretty good guess. 'Your mother's behind it,' she told him. 'That's what started Beth off – her dying when she was so young. Then you get dragged in because you have the same trauma. She was your mother too after all.'

Louis groaned. 'We saw that thing,' he insisted. 'It didn't look anything like our mother!'

'Well, she wouldn't, would she? She's been dead for fourteen years,' pointed out Ivan.

'I wasn't saying the monster was Beth's mother, you morons,' said Coll. 'I'm saying that losing her so early is what's behind Beth's trauma. None of you saw anything – you just think you did. It's not an exorcist you need, it's a counsellor. I keep saying this. Beth, you need to talk to someone who knows how to deal with the psychology going on here, not this pair of over-suggestible nitwits.'

'I tried it,' Beth said.

'What about Ivan?' asked Louis. 'He saw it too.'

'Yeah, but Ivan's an idiot,' explained Coll. 'If we all said we saw a talking furball in the corner he'd not only start seeing it himself, he'd probably try to date it as well.'

It was a stand-off.

'Sorry. It's against all my principles to believe in monsters,' Coll insisted.

'OK,' said Louis. 'But the fact is, *we* believe it. Right?'

Coll rolled her eyes. The whole thing was making her furious. 'This is your *sister*, Louis! How you can you be so stupid? I just don't get it.'

'You weren't there, I was,' he said defensively. 'Anyway, look. The idea is, we need to go back to that house and check it out. And we need you to help us.'

'I suppose it'll prove to you it's not real,' said Coll. 'Tell you what. I'll come — so long as you both agree to go to a counsellor after.'

'We don't want you to come,' said Louis. 'What we want — just to keep us happy, OK? — is for you to do some research for us. Find out exactly what this thing is.'

'And how to kill it,' said Ivan.

'You can't do research into something that doesn't exist,' Coll pointed out.

'Just for us,' said Beth. 'For me. This is your area, Coll. We don't know where to start. Just — spend a couple of days helping us out. OK?'

Coll paused. 'I don't think I ought to be going along with this. You need help, but not from me.'

'You're scared,' said Ivan.

'Please. Save me the cheap psychological tricks. Do I look like a bloke?'

'Yep.'

'Stop it, you two,' begged Beth. 'You'll help us find out, won't you? Please, Coll?'

Coll sighed — and gave in. 'OK. But one thing — I *am* coming with you. Letting you guys loose in a darkened room at the moment would be like leaving a bunch of agoraphobes out on the high wire. You need me there to hold your hands. Deal?'

'Deal.'

✶

Colette was a rationalist. She didn't think that science knew everything but she did believe that, in theory, it could. The universe was forever changing: science was an endless quest to try and understand it. But some things had already been established. Light travelled at a certain speed, the Earth went round the sun – and the dead could no more come back to life than a dog could make a decent cheese toastie. Facts were facts. That was one of them.

She had not completely dismissed the idea that her friends were trying to set her up with some prank or other. People were always winding her up about her screwy brain, and she could kind of see how they might want to trick her into believing that the ghosties were coming. But she thought it unlikely. Ivan, perhaps, but neither Beth nor Louis were the kind to go to such lengths just to make a fool of her – especially her Bethie. No; they were off on one. Beth had always been a little . . . what was the word? Not odd. Odd wasn't a word Coll would use about anyone just because they were different. Strange. She was deep in unexpected ways. She was always coming up with odd remarks and ideas that seemed to come from nowhere, and which seemed to surprise her as much as they did anyone else. It was a part of her friend that Coll could never predict or understand.

She was deeply disappointed in Louis for getting sucked in, though. She'd thought he was too sensible for this kind of nonsense. Still, if playing along with it was the way to get them the help they needed then she was happy to do it.

She knew exactly the place Beth, Ivan and Louis would want her to go: the Collesbrooke, a library not far south of Manchester. It had been founded by the infamous Elizabethan magician Dr John Dee and specialised in all things supernatural. Used by generations of occultists, devil worshippers, sorcerers, resurrectionists, alchemists, witches and other fakers and self-deluders, some of the volumes there went back centuries. If you wanted to learn about the occult, that was the place to go.

Coll dismissed it at once. She wasn't planning to do any serious research into the history of bullshit. She just wanted something that fitted the bill well enough to convince her friends. She could have gone online and collected any amount of nonsense for them, but she figured that what they really needed wasn't just bullshit, it was *old* bullshit. People from the past wrote just as much crap then as they did now – more, in her opinion – but crap aged well. A pile of supernatural shite written down a couple of hundred years ago read so much better than the identical shite written down the day before

yesterday. Old paper. A bit of bookworm . . . Bingo!
It must be true.

There was another resource much closer to hand –
a run-down old shop tucked away behind the
Arndale centre in Manchester, just a bus ride away. It
sold mainly cheap second-hand paperbacks, a little
vintage porn, a few remaindered hardbacks, vinyl,
CDs and so on. Cheap and tatty today, it had at one
time been a thriving second-hand bookshop, selling a
wide range of old books, including some collectors'
and antiquarian stuff. There were still a few of these
left over from the glory days. The collectors had
moved on, and the vintage titles were left stranded
there among the cheap detective thrillers, romances
and porn.

Jack, the owner, remembered Coll from earlier in
the year when she'd come in poking about for a
history project she was doing. It had been Jack's part-
ner, an older man, who had run the shop originally.
He'd died years before and Jack himself didn't have
the interest, the energy or the knowledge to go
hunting for antiquarian stock. But he missed the
gentle and eccentric customers from the old days. He
was pleased to see Coll again, and he followed her to
the back of the shop where the old stock was kept.
There were only a couple of shelves left and it took
her just a few minutes to rifle through them, looking

for something that she remembered from before. And there it was — *The Supernatural: A Natural History of the Impossible* by B. R. Jonstone. Cloth-bound, published in 1856.

She was bound to find some suitable tripe in that one.

'Ah, yes, Jonstone! Quite a well-known figure in his day — did a lot of good work digging up old legends and stories,' lied Jack hopefully.

'It looks a little populist for what I'm after,' said Coll, bargaining already as she flicked through the pages. Ah — there it was: 'Ghouls and their Relatives'. Perfect.

'Not many copies left, I would imagine,' said Jack. 'The price will be out of date by now,' he added, peering over her shoulder to try and see what was written in pencil on the flyleaf.

'I don't see why, if he was so well known. It's not even a first edition,' said Coll firmly.

'This was one of his lesser-known works,' said Jack.

'Worth even less then. A fiver?' said Coll.

'A fiver? Don't make me laugh! I couldn't let it go for under thirty pounds, and that's cheap,' said Jack indignantly.

'Nah, too much. Thanks, anyway,' said Coll, and snapped the book shut. She got it for fifteen pounds in the end – a bargain. She walked to the stop, got on her bus, and started to read through.

It was interesting stuff, the history of the Ghoul. According to Jonstone the ghoul myth had originated in the deserts of Arabia, where they sometimes took on the form of hyenas. No doubt it was the sight of these beasts hanging around grave-yards looking for human carrion that had started off the whole story.

Killing a ghoul, as you might expect for something that was never truly alive in the first place, was simply not enough. The usual course of events, of course, after capturing one, was to kill it, bury it in the local graveyard and forget about it.

Mistake. Death didn't actually do them all that much harm at all. The creature would simply wake up underground, burrow its way out and then carry on feasting on the rotting flesh of its graveyard com-panions as if it had suffered nothing worse than a slight headache.

Worse than that. Your ghoul, it appeared, was not only capable of dropping in and out of death as if it were just popping down to the corner shop for a pint of milk; it could regenerate its entire body from the smallest fragments. A finger could turn into the whole beast within a few days. Even teeth, according to Jonstone, had been known to regenerate back into the complete entity, given time. Shooting, stabbing, hanging, that sort of thing, hardly gave it pause. No, the only way to make sure a ghoul was destroyed was to burn it to ashes – so thoroughly that not even a fragment of toenail remained.

Tricky. On the other hand there were a number of other techniques that would knock it back for long enough to cart it off to the local incinerator before it came back to life. Jonstone had very kindly written a list of them down. They included:

Exposure to sunlight.

Stake through the heart.

Tear out the creature's heart and place a crucifix in the cavity.

('Ew,' muttered Coll.)

Drown it in holy water.

Bury it at a crossroads.

Bury it with a virgin at midnight.

'Jesus,' said Coll. One minute it was nearly inde-structible, the next you could immobilise it with a sun lamp. It was the most amazing blither she'd ever read. For a moment she doubted that her friends would be taken in by it; but then she read the final entry.

If it should be felt impractical to tend a fire so well as to render even the bones to ashes, another method may be employed, which although it will not kill the fiend may paralyse it and leave it in the ground for ever. It should be buried with a brick inserted in the mouth, inscribed with the following spell: 'To one who is alive, let there be always life; to one who is dead, let there be an eternal hunger.'

'For the living, life; for the dead, the hunger that never ends,' Coll murmured. It was the exact same phrase — a weaker translation than Beth's, but the original Latin had undoubtedly been the same.

'Fascinating!' she exclaimed out loud. It seemed as if her friends were not the only ones to swallow this nonsense whole. In which case, she realised with a start, at least part of what they had told her might be true. Someone may have actually taken that brick from the tomb of a Roman ghoul and used it to inter it again over here, back in Jacobean times. But why dig it up in the first place? To study it? To kill it properly? Not to liberate it, surely?

Astonishing! So this ridiculous belief had persisted for all that time! A Roman ghoul, buried for over two thousand years, had just been released again and was busy gobbling its way back to health. It was almost a pity it wasn't true.

Was it known in the academic community, she wondered, that these beliefs were so old? There was a paper here for her to write, perhaps. Coll hugged her book. Out of stupidity came forth knowledge, she thought. Maybe there was something interesting buried among all this bullshit after all.

Chapter Seven

Coll delivered her side of the bargain that same day.

'Tomorrow, then,' said Louis.

'Why not tonight?' said Coll. 'Get it done.'

'We need to prepare,' said Beth.

'Yeah. We go armed,' said Ivan.

'Sunlight's my favourite,' suggested Coll. 'Trap it in a room with a boxed set of *Friends* so it forgets the passage of time — then pull the curtains open suddenly. Frazzle!' She gave them her most winsome smile. 'Still believe me? And if you do — are you stupid enough to go back there?'

'We don't have any choice,' Louis said.

'If it's a ghoul you need to burn it to stop it for good. To ashes. Even a tooth can regenerate. I can't believe you guys are swallowing this drivel,' Coll added, shaking her head.

'What about the brick?' said Ivan. 'I like the brick.' He made a motion of smashing the brick down into the creature's face.

'OK,' said Coll. 'Let's get ready. What sort of preparation do you need to do? Rub a clove of garlic on the Bible and off we go. Where is this place, anyway?' she asked.

Louis shook his head. 'Wait till tomorrow,' he said. 'See how you feel about it after that.'

Coll shrugged. 'Please yourself. Ghoul hunt! Should be fun, huh?'

For Beth, perhaps the most important news Coll had brought them was about the brick. No doubt she, Beth, had taken it from the creature's throat when she had dug it up, releasing it. So long as they had the brick they possessed the means of putting the ghoul back in the ground, where it belonged. How she had known to take it back home with her, or why the creature had allowed it, she did not know – but it was certainly coming with them when they returned. If the ghoul was still there – weakened, perhaps, by Ivan's attack – there was a chance that they could undo the damage there and then.

None of them were taking any chances. If they were going, they were going armed to the teeth.

Jonstone had mentioned staking – stabbing the thing through its heart, if it had one. That had to be good. But what with? Beth and Louis's dad had been doing some DIY jobs for them around the house a while ago and there were some tools still lying around. They took a nice big chisel, plus knives, skewers, hammers and a Stanley knife. Ivan even took the corkscrew.

'What are you going to do, drink him to death?' asked Coll.

'Go for the eyes,' said Ivan, making a stabbing movement with the corkscrew. 'You never know.'

'If it is a ghoul, it might not go for you at all. They're supposed to like their food dead, aren't they?' she pointed out.

'Yeah, well, this one seems to like preparing its food first,' said Ivan.

Beth stuck more or less to the things Coll had suggested – stabbers and fire, and of course, the brick, as well as practical things such as torches and matches. But the boys got right into it. Louis had gone for the religious paraphernalia. A Bible, of course, a couple of crucifixes.

'You're wasting space,' scoffed Ivan. He'd taken inspiration from the movies instead – garlic, a cross, even a silver letter-opener. 'Not bullets but better than nothing in a tight corner,' he said.

Coll peered into his rucksack. 'It looks like a charity-shop bag,' she said. 'What's he going to do, root through the second-hand books while you peel the garlic?'

Having Coll around was good – she brought some humour to the situation. But Beth had serious doubts about involving her. Later, when her friend went off to work in her room, she had it out with Louis and Ivan.

'It's not fair,' she said. 'She doesn't know the whole story. We shouldn't put her in danger.'

'We told her most of it,' said Ivan. There was one bit they had left out – where Ivan had beaten the ghoul's head to a pulp. He was still afraid that he might have committed murder.

'That's not the point,' said Beth. 'She doesn't believe it. That means she doesn't know what she's letting herself in for.'

There was a grim silence. Louis nodded. 'We can't bring her,' he agreed.

Ivan didn't like it, but none of them, not even him, were ruthless enough to put her in the same danger they were in. They decided to go that same night, and somehow dodge Coll.

It was after nine by the time they'd finished their

preparations. Louis suggested going out for a drink. Coll agreed — she thought it might help them take their minds off how mad they all were — and suggested a quiet pub across the road. The other three fancied somewhere with a bit of life, though, and they ended up in a busy student bar on the Wilmslow Road. Coll stuck to them like glue, but eventually, after several drinks, she had to go to the loo. They managed to slip out and head off down the road towards the ruined house without being spotted.

Ivan set off in front, at a gallop.

'What's the rush?' asked Beth.

'Midnight. I don't want to be doing this during the witching hour. Think about it.'

Louis looked at his watch. 'It's quarter to eleven.' The house was about half an hour away.

'Come on — run!' said Ivan. He shot off down the road, and they had to race to keep up with him.

666

The derelict house was one of a row of four that had been earmarked for demolition and redevelopment years ago. With the recession, work had been delayed and was unlikely to start any time soon. No one else had been inside for years.

They paused outside and looked up at it. Their

memories of what had happened last time stared balefully back down at them.

'Well? Are we going in or not?' said Beth.

Ivan looked up at the house, his face grey in the orange lamplight. 'Do you know what?' he said. 'I don't think we are.'

'Ivan—' began Louis.

'In the dark?' said Ivan. 'At midnight? If we have to do this, let's do it in daylight. I mean, for God's sake.'

Louis winced. 'It's a point,' he admitted. 'The darkness is his, isn't it?' His voice faded away. They stood still, looking up. The house loomed over them like some tottering, cancerous giant, full of death. Around them, the deep shadows in the windows hid God knew what secrets. They had all been taught when they were small that the darkness had nothing in it. Now they knew better.

Beth shuddered.

'You OK?' asked Louis.

She felt inside her mind. It felt clean. She nodded. 'I'm OK,' she said.

Louis looked at her carefully. 'You sure?'

She felt again, carefully, slowly, for any slight sign. Nothing. 'I'm sure,' she said.

And as soon as she spoke she realised that she wasn't all right at all. Something was there: it had been hiding, but now . . .

She tried to open her mouth, but couldn't. The darkness rushed out from within and seized hold of her. The stink of death filled her body and mind; she would have retched but she was unable to move a muscle. Then it came upon her tenfold – hunger, hunger! It filled her body and soul. She began to scream, but was unable to make the slightest noise.

'Let's go round the back anyway, and take a look,' she heard a voice saying. It was hers.

'What for?' said Ivan. 'If we're not going in . . .'

'We need to discuss it. But not here.' Her head moved, looking up and down the road. Hungry, said a voice inside her. Hungry, Beth. Hungry.

'Let's just go down here,' she said. Her foot moved. Behind her eyes, she looked out. None of them had any idea what was happening to her. It's not me! It's not me! she wanted to yell. Silently, she led them down the alley to the back of the house.

It all looked the same at the back – same rubbish, same window, same dirty concrete yard.

'OK,' said Louis. 'So what do we do now?'

'You know what?' Beth said. 'I think it's OK. He's not here any more. I'd know it if he was.'

'And the bodies?' asked Ivan, nodding at the

ramshackle building. 'Are they still there? Can you tell?'

Beth, paralysed, shook her head. 'We need to go in and see,' she said. It was so like her voice! Not quite, but so close. Good enough to fool the boys, anyway.

Louis paused. He licked his lips and nodded. 'Get it over with,' he said.

'But not me,' said Beth.

They both turned to look at her. They had agreed they must stick together.

'How come?' said Ivan.

'I can't,' she murmured. Tears sprang into her eyes. She lifted up her face so that they could see them glistening. She smiled bravely. 'Too scared,' she confessed. 'Sorry, I can't do it, Lou. That's all there is to it. I'm sorry. I'm really sorry. I thought I was strong enough but I'm not.'

'You were so keen just now,' said Ivan, looking curiously at her.

This is not me! screamed Beth from inside the dungeon of her head. 'Got lost somewhere,' she whispered pathetically.

Ivan looked up at the house and winced.

Louis licked his lips nervously. 'No splitting up, that's what we said,' he pointed out. 'And anyway – why can't it wait till tomorrow?'

'Ivan can wait with me.'

'No way,' said Ivan quickly. 'Louis – don't do it.' He looked at Beth and shook his head. 'He's your brother,' he told her. 'You want to send your brother in there on his own?'

Beth looked straight back at him. She could feel it – him – she realised, daring Ivan to see through her.

'But that thing's not there any more. Like I said, I know it – I can feel it. Whatever it was, it's gone. But the bodies may still be there, I think. One of us should go in. It's the only way to find out.'

'It's not there but you're too scared to go?'

'The bodies,' Beth whispered. 'I killed a man. I can't—'

And at that moment there came a chilling sound from near the house. It was a guttural and inhuman noise, rising to an ear-splitting shriek, before catching on itself and dying on a strangled choke. It shattered the fetid stillness around them like a hammer blow. All three leapt into the air and tumbled backwards, gasping with fear.

Something was advancing at them up the alley by the side of the building. They backed away, but came up against the heap of rubble in the yard.

They were trapped.

A shape staggered towards them out of the darkness. Louis fumbled in his backpack for his weapons.

The monster took another step closer. It waved its arms in the air and snarled at them.

'Behold!' it roared. 'I am the Zombie Princess.'

Pause.

'You fucking bitch!' yelled Ivan. 'Jesus! Jesus! My chest nearly bloody exploded!'

'Christ, Coll – you cow!' groaned Louis.

Beth stood still and watched, an odd half-smile on her face. 'You made me jump,' she said.

Coll had seen straight through them, of course. She had waited in hiding outside the pub, followed them and picked her moment perfectly. When things had calmed down and the boys told her they were changing their minds, she sneered knowingly.

'You bunch of wimps,' she said.

Ivan shook his head. 'We only came tonight to save you, but you know where the house is now. Let's come back tomorrow when we can see what we're doing.'

'Oh, come on,' jeered Coll. 'Now's the ideal time. Tell you what – *I'll* go first if you like.'

'You don't know what's in there,' said Louis. He looked at Ivan. Maybe they ought to tell her that something – or someone – had its brains beaten out up there. But Ivan shook his head.

Coll was disgused. 'Christ, you guys really do believe this stuff, don't you?'

'We need to find out,' said Beth. 'Louis, take Coll. I'll stay here with Ivan.'

Coll frowned and peered at her. 'Where's my brave Beth?' she asked. Inside her skull, Beth screamed: See me, hear me! It's not me! But not a note escaped her. Instead, she just shook her head and looked ashamed.

Ivan grabbed Louis by the arm. 'Don't go, man,' he said. 'Whatever's up there, you don't want to see it.'

'I'm going even if I have to go on my own,' announced Coll. 'You guys can come or not, as you like.'

She turned and walked towards the building. 'Up this pipe, yeah?'

Louis clutched his head. He wanted to help Beth, but why make plans only to change them?

'Go on,' Beth urged him. 'You know where it is.'

Coll began heaving herself up the pipe and Louis hurried after her. He waited till she reached the top, then scrambled up himself, fighting against the overwhelming feeling that this was wrong, so wrong. But it was too late now. He paused at the top to take out his torch, and looked back at Beth and Ivan on the ground below him.

'Stay with her this time, OK?' he ordered Ivan. Louis peered back inside the building. It was pitch black. He turned on his torch and followed Coll in through the open window.

Ivan watched him disappear. He was astonished. They had all agreed to stay together. *Now* look!

'How did this happen? How come you wanted him to go?' he asked Beth.

She shrugged lightly, as if it was nothing to do with her. 'He's gone,' she said. 'It's quite safe.'

She moved away from the house into the deeper shadows at the back of the yard. Nervously, Ivan followed her.

'How do you know?'

Beth took him by the hand. Stay away from me! she screamed silently. Don't, Ivan . . . please, don't! He thought Louis was in danger. In fact, it was *him*.

'You haven't been anywhere near me lately,' she said softly. So clever! she thought. So – clever, so deadly. Was she really going to have to stand there and watch? She heaved and strained against her muscles, but they were in the grip of a will stronger than hers.

Ivan looked at her in surprise. 'It hasn't kinda been the time, you know?'

Beth stood there in the dark, waiting. He reached out and touched her on the arm. 'I still think you're gorgeous, though,' he whispered. He ran his hand down to hers and squeezed it. She squeezed back, lifting up her face. Ivan stepped closer, still unsure.

'But is this the right time?' he asked. It had never been a worse time. Beth pulled him close and Ivan went in for a kiss. She stroked his neck. He ran his hand under her coat and touched her breast. Unseen by him, a tear escaped from her eye and crept down her face. Like a princess in a fairy tale, one tear was all she could shed.

'I think I might have fallen in love with you,' said Ivan.

With no apparent effort, Beth lifted him from the ground by the neck. Ivan gurgled and kicked, his shoes banging against her shins, so she slammed him to the ground, sat on top of him, wrapped both hands firmly around his neck and squeezed. Ivan's neck was yielding but tough, like some kind of warm root in her hands. He clawed at her hands, struggling like a child, his eyes bulging in disbelief. His windpipe cracked with a small sound like breaking plastic. Desperately, Beth tried to unlock her hands – or at least to turn her head away so that she didn't have to watch. Close my eyes, close my eyes! she begged. But the force inside her was dominant. It fixed her stare on Ivan's face and made her watch the whole thing, in terrifying detail – the swollen face, the bulging eyes, the protruding tongue, right up to the last twitch.

You'd have thought it would be better with a torch, but in some ways it was even worse, thought Louis.

Whenever he moved, the shadows pounced and swam around him like living things. Not nice. He followed Coll to the bottom of the stairs. Already he could smell the stink.

Coll paused. 'Something's dead,' she said. In the darkness she turned to him. 'Louis, what happened in here?'

'I was attacked,' he said. 'Beth was possessed. That's the only way to describe it. We fought it off.' He stood behind her, panting with fear. 'Ivan got it with a wooden beam.'

Coll froze. 'What do you mean, he got it with a beam? You didn't hurt anyone, did you, Louis?'

'We didn't mean to. It's not human, Coll! If it's here, you'll see.'

'Christ. Now I am scared.' Coll moved closer to him.

'You shouldn't be here,' Louis said. 'This is just between the three of us.'

'Too late now,' said Coll. She paused a moment longer. The house shifted around them; the darkness drew breath. It stank to high heaven.

'OK,' said Coll. 'That's enough. Let's go.'

Suddenly the two of them were running for their lives. They arrived at the window at the same moment and tried to get down together, but their combined weight was too much for the pipe and it gave way.

Down they went, crashing onto the heap of rubbish in the yard below, bruised and squealing with fear. Louis was first to his feet, jumping up to check up at the window.

There was nothing to be seen.

Coll groaned. Still sitting on the ground, she put her hand to her mouth and laughed weakly.

'That was fucking stupid,' cursed Louis. Ahead of him, Beth stepped forward out of the shadows at the end of the yard.

Louis looked around. 'Where's Ivan?'

'He heard something and went round the front to see.'

Louis was furious. 'He left you on your own? Again? Are you OK?'

'I'm OK,' she said. Not. Not.

'Yup, and me, I'm fine too, thanks, a broken arse is just what I wanted,' said Coll, limping over to them.

'Louis . . .' whispered Beth.

'You weren't even supposed to be here,' said Louis to Coll. 'We were trying to do you a favour.'

'Ok, fuck this,' snapped Coll. 'I was stupid to let myself get dragged in. I'm going home.'

She turned and stamped up the alley to the street, with Louis and Beth behind her. The road was empty.

'Where's he gone? Don't say he's gone home,' said

Louis. He took a few steps up the road to search for him when Coll said, 'Beth? What is it?' Louis turned round to look.

His sister seemed to be having some sort of slow-motion fit on the road behind them. The enemy inside her was weakening. She could feel it. Inch by inch she was trying to move back into herself, to repossess her muscles and her mind. As Louis and Coll had tumbled out of the window, she had managed to move a finger. In the yard she had slipped odd words out of her mouth. But now, as they came into the street, she was finally able to try and seize full control. But he was still fighting.

Louis ran up to her. 'What is it? Is it him? It is, isn't it?' he begged.

Beth began to jerk spastically, trying to force him out of herself – too late for Ivan, but for herself, for her friends, for them all. Louis grabbed hold of her coat and shook her.

'What's going on?' he demanded. 'Leave her alone! In the name of God – go!'

'He . . . Grnnnn,' Beth grunted, forcing words into her mouth. She twisted her head. He was going – fleeing to his own body. And he was near . . . right here.

'Him,' she said. She shook her head. 'There. Him.' She inclined her head sideways. Louis followed her movement to the shadows at the side of the house. But there was nothing to see.

And then he was gone, flung out into the air. Beth sank to her knees, Louis holding on to her. 'He's there – there! That's him. See?' she said. Then she gasped: 'Louis, he made me kill Ivan.'

Something moved in the shadows of the old building. A tramp. He limped out of a doorway into the light. Louis stepped between him and Beth, slung his rucksack off his shoulder and took out a long, sharp kitchen knife.

'Louis, what the fuck?' yelled Coll.

Louis ignored her. He stepped closer to the tramp. 'Who are you?' he demanded.

The figure didn't answer, just stood there, his face obscured by a scarf wrapped around it. He was trembling from head to foot like an old, old man.

'Who are you?' Louis said again.

The man spoke. 'You sister,' he said uncertainly. He spoke with an accent, but it was like nothing they had ever heard before. 'You sister . . . she not well. She need help. Sick, very sick.'

'Who are you?'

'Dangerous,' said the figure. 'I think she come here many times. I see her. She try to kill—'

'Not me!' shouted Beth. 'Not me – you!'

She ran forward. She could feel him pulling at her

legs, but it was tired; it had overreached itself. At last, she was the stronger of the two. This was their chance. Louis grabbed at her arm and but she slipped past him and ran at the tramp. She pushed him hard in the chest with both hands, so that he tumbled down and hit the road, clutching the scarf to his face.

'Beth!' shrieked Coll, shocked. 'What are you doing?'

'He can't hurt us, he's weak,' shouted Beth. 'He needs someone else's strength to do his work.' She knelt down and seized the old man around the neck. 'Louis! We have him. Help me, help me!' she cried.

Louis ran up and lifted up his knife.

'In Jesus's name, die!' he shouted. But then he paused. Louis was strong, but he was a gentle boy. He had never killed before – he had never even been in a fight. Even so, it was not his courage but his conscience that failed him. To take a life! He wavered, the knife held high above his head, the creature's coal black eyes staring up at him. Louis bared his teeth, raised the knife another inch and prepared to bring it down . . .

The blow never landed. Coll ran at him, shoving him to one side. Louis fell, sprawling on the ground next to Beth and the old man.

'You guys are off your heads,' yelled Coll.

'Coll, it's real – help us, please help us,' Beth

begged. She seized hold of the tramp's neck again but Coll was pulling at her hair to get her off him. Beth fell back and kicked out at his face as Coll dragged her backwards. But Louis pushed Coll away and struggled with her as Beth launched herself forward again. She had the tramp in her grip again. She was wrestling with him, desperately trying to seize his neck and strangle him. She pulled at the scarf covering his face and stared wildly at what was beneath. Then . . . 'What did you make me do?' she cried. 'What did you make me do?' She began to beat the back of the old man's head against the pavement – a terrible thing to watch, a strong young woman beating a helpless old man. 'You made me . . . you made me . . .' she screamed.

Coll escaped Louis's grasp and ran forward. For the first time she clearly saw the face of the tramp by the light of the street lamps – and fell to her knees in shock at the sight.

The thing had grown. There was more flesh now, some of it living, some dead; some decaying, some still leathery and mummified. It had a face. The bone was completely covered, the eyes bright. In places you could see the blood moving under the papery skin. But it stank – oh, how it stank – of rotten flesh, of death. It *was* death. Only now the death was fresher.

Coll screamed, a terrible, hysterical noise, and

scrambled backwards on her hands and feet to get away from it.

'*Non potes me pellere,*' cried the creature. '*Ego sum immortalis.*' Then; 'Help me, help me . . .'

Louis ran forward and Coll snatched out at him, still trying to hold him and Beth back. For a moment they were all fighting amongst themselves; but then from the creature on the ground there came a sound that Louis had heard once before in the derelict house – part snarl, part laugh, part mad scream. It made the hair on their heads stand on end. Under Beth's hands, the thing's neck swelled and thickened. There was fur.

Coll screamed again in a panic at the impossible. A thick-necked head swivelled round and they were looking into the eyes of a dog. No – a wolf. No – something else . . .

Whatever it was, it was half-dead. Like the tramp's, its face was rotting.

The thing snarled and snapped at them. They fell back.

'Hyena!' yelled Louis. 'Hyena!'

The animal was huge, waist-high at the shoulders. It snapped at Louis, caught his sleeve in its teeth and shook its head like a dog with a toy. Louis flapped like a rag and dropped to his knees. Coll ran round behind it and kicked the creature hard, between the legs; her speciality. The beast yelped and scuttled off, its back legs doubling under it in pain. Louis staggered a few steps after it but it was already too late. It was still weak; but a wounded hyena was a very different thing from a wounded old man. Swaying with weakness, and looking half-human in the lamplight, it ran up the road on its long forelegs, swerving in between the parked cars. It paused, glanced behind at them, then ran around a corner and was gone. A moment later they heard it call again – that bizarre, savage, laughing yelp.

There was a shocked silence. Beth and Louis were still on the ground. Coll, on her feet, made a whimpering noise, like a puppy.

They had missed their chance.

Beth pulled herself up onto her hands and knees. Louis was sitting up, examining his arm. His jacket was in tatters.

'You OK?' she asked.

'Think so. You?'

She nodded and tried to calm her breathing. 'Louis, I tried to tell you. I was there all the time. It made me watch.'

'Don't.'

'I should have—'

'Don't.'

'What was it?' said Coll. 'It changed, didn't it? I saw it change from a man into . . .' No one replied. 'I'm sorry,' said Coll. 'I'm really sorry,' She burst into hysterical tears, sobbing and shaking. Beth crawled over to comfort her.

Louis came to join them and for a moment they sat still, kneeling in the road, embracing, waiting for Coll to calm down.

'Jesus,' she said at last, still panting and shaking like a leaf. 'I went into that house. And you came with me.'

'Yeah,' said Louis. 'But it was out here all the time.' He sighed and looked at Beth. 'So, what about Ivan?' he said.

Beth led them back to the courtyard behind the house where she had left him. As they entered the cluttered yard there was a noise in the darkness and they froze. Something big was scrambling clumsily up the pile of rubbish at the back of the yard.

Beth called out 'Ivan! Ivan!' Whatever it was, it paused at the top of the heap. Maybe it turned its head, but in that light it was impossible to make out anything except shadows and darker shadows. They were certain it was their enemy. But why had he come back here?

In the darkness, it jumped down. They heard it

land on the pavement on the other side and run off. Beth ran over to dig in the spot where she had hidden Ivan's body after he had stopped moving, but there was no sign of him. They all joined in, pulling away at the rubbish. There was nothing there.

Ivan was lost.

Chapter Eight

Back at home, Beth ran straight upstairs. Louis, on her case all the way, wanted to know where she was going.

'The toilet,' she snapped. 'I have my period, OK?'

That headed him off. Louis went to the kitchen. He paused at the door.

'I'm putting the kettle on. You'll be down, will you?'

'When I'm done,' Beth said. She waited till she heard the kitchen door close behind him, then went into the bathroom.

This had to stop. The grave had been enough, but this? First the counsellor, now Ivan. Two lives already. Who would be next? Louis? Coll? Her father?

It was in her power to stop this once and for all.

She went to the bathroom cabinet and searched through. Two packets of paracetamol and one of aspirin. She hadn't had time to think it through. Damn it! She could go to the garage up the road and get some more pills there, but they never sold you more than one packet at a time.

How many did you need?

There might be some in the kitchen, but she couldn't go down there with Louis and Coll about. Beth tiptoed into Ivan's room and found another half-pack of paracetamol and a half-bottle of vodka. Her stash was growing. If she went to the garage up the road she could buy more . . . and there was another garage further off by Owens Park . . . and maybe one of the student late shops.

It might be enough. She couldn't do it here, anyway. They'd find her and stop her. Where, then, in a busy city? There were some allotments not far off. She could sit herself down behind someone's shed, drink the vodka, swallow the pills and stop this now, before anyone else died.

A place to die.

'It's not you,' Louis had said. But it was her hands doing the killing. She could feel Ivan's throat right now, how it had pulsed beneath her fingers as she'd squeezed the life out of him. How heavy his body had become, and how still, when the life had gone. Any further lives would be on her conscience. She could turn herself in to the police, of course, but even if she was convicted, what would that mean? Life in a cell, waiting for that thing to turn up inside her again and use her eyes, her ears, her hands, her mouth, to do whatever it chose?

No. There was only one sentence for her: death.

Beth hurried along the landing just as the door opened downstairs and Coll put her head out of the kitchen.

'Beth? You OK?'

'Fine. I'm just coming.'

She went into her room and quietly locked the door. There was no chance of getting out downstairs – they'd be certain to hear her. She had to escape! She spilled the pills onto her bed. She had maybe thirty. Was it enough?

She picked up a handful and opened the half-bottle of vodka. She lifted it up – and something seized hold of her throat.

It was coming.

'No, not now, not now.' Here, in the house, with Louis and Coll? It wanted them, too? Desperately she fumbled at the cardboard cartons and foil packets, ripping at them and stuffing the pills into her mouth. She got seven or eight in and tried to swallow, but her throat closed up and refused to accept them. She fell down on the bed on all fours and tried to force her gullet to obey her.

A voice in her head. 'Let me in. Beth — let me in!'

She started to try and force the pills down with her fingers but only made herself retch. A power within her seized her hands, her throat, her mouth . . .

'Not like this,' cried a voice. 'Let me in. Let me in! Let me in, Beth.'

Already she was unable to move, already her body was not her own. She opened her mouth to scream and the pills fell out onto the duvet. Deep inside her, something began to rise to the surface.

There was a minute or more as Beth lay on the bed, her teeth grinding and muscles twitching. Then she relaxed quite suddenly and went to the mirror.

'There now. There. Look at you! Look at you . . .' she said. She sighed, moved closer to the mirror, and smiled. 'Ain't you pretty?' she said; and she began to cry.

It was ten more minutes before Coll went up to check that Beth was all right. She found the toilet unoccupied and Beth's door locked. She called. No answer, but inside the room she heard voices.

Beth was not alone.

'Louis! Get up here – quick!'

Louis raced up the stairs three at a time and banged on the door.

'Beth! What's going on?'

There was no answer. He jumped back and flung himself at the door. But the landlord had conscientiously fitted solid fire doors and good locks from the inside. He just bounced back.

Leaving Louis to bruise his shoulders on the door, Coll ran downstairs to fetch some tools. She came back armed with a chisel and a lump hammer. Louis seized the hammer from her and began pounding at the lock, but after a couple of blows he was stopped by a voice from inside.

'Louis. Stop.'

It was a woman's voice – and it was not Beth's.

'Open it,' he cried.

'The lock will be released,' said the voice. Almost at once they heard the mechanism moving in the wood.

'The door will open,' said the voice. The handle moved down and the door swung quietly open.

There was no one behind it. Beth was sitting in her work chair, facing the bed. As they came in, she turned to look at them, her eyes wide open, and she began to speak to herself in two clearly separate voices.

'Who is it?

'It's Louis.

'Louis . . .'

She smiled at him and shook her head sadly. Louis began to tremble uncontrollably.

'Does he know?

'No more than I do.

'I don't have long. Sorry, Louis, so sorry . . .

'No, no, you're slipping away, concentrate, concentrate on me. You have to tell me before you go.

'I'm trying. It's so hard, it's so hard to be here . . .'

Beth turned away and continued the twofold conversation with herself in a low whisper, leaving Louis and Coll standing by the door, excluded. There was no doubt about it. At this moment in time, Beth was two separate people.

'Jesus Christ, that's spooky,' hissed Coll. 'Listen to her! Who the fuck is she talking to?'

Louis scowled and bent his head to one side. It was sending shivers up and down his spine. 'Right,' he said. 'This has gone on long enough.'

He walked across to Beth and bent down to shake her. As soon as he touched her, her eyes snapped open and her stare fixed on him.

'Louis,' the woman's voice said, as clear as day. He jumped back as if he had been shocked. 'Stop that,' the voice continued. 'Leave me with her.'

'Who are you?'

'You know who I am.'

'Christ on a bike,' hissed Coll. 'Who is it? What's going on? This is spooking me out.'

Beth kept her eyes fixed directly on Louis. 'You know me, Louis. Don't you?'

Louis swallowed. To his own surprise, he felt like weeping. 'I *don't* know you,' he said. Then, more loudly. 'Leave my sister alone. In Jesus's name . . .'

Beth sat up in her chair. 'You know me,' she cried. 'Louis! What's wrong with you? Can't you recognise your own mother? Leave us now. Go!'

Louis staggered back, dumbstruck. But it was right. He knew – as soon as he'd heard her voice, he'd known. He just hadn't been able to let himself believe it. His beloved mother, dead all these years, had come back to see his sister – and to send him away. Pushing Coll aside, he rushed out of the room. Beth sank back down and continued her strange two-way conversation, her eyes moving from side to side as she spoke. Coll stood over her indecisively for a moment. Then, abruptly, Beth sighed, closed her eyes, and relaxed. Coll waited a few seconds longer, but it was over. Beth was asleep.

She went downstairs to look for Louis.

✼

She found him sitting at the kitchen table. She stood next to him, unsure of what to do. 'You want a drink?' she asked.

'We got any beer?'

Coll went to the fridge and found a can. 'We'll have to share. Ivan's had the rest, as usual.' She opened the beer, took a swig and plonked it down in front of him. 'So was that who she said she was?'

Louis sighed and wiped his eyes on his sleeve. 'It was just like her. The way she moved, the way she smiled. She's been dead for fourteen years.' His voice cracked.

Coll put her hand on his shoulder. Louis shook his head and began to leak tears. 'She sent me away,' he wept.

'Not very motherly,' agreed Coll, and took another swig of beer. 'I expect she was busy, though, you know? Being dead.'

'Did I do the right thing?' Louis asked. 'Leaving her, I mean?'

Coll was watching her hand, which had started to shake. 'I don't know,' she said. 'They didn't teach us this stuff at school. My God. My whole world just fell to bits.' She shook her head. Her voice was shaking as well. 'Bloody dead people,' she added. 'You put them in the ground, you fill in. Do they stay put? No, they do not.' She stretched the word 'not' out, just to listen to her voice quavering.

Louis forced a wry smile, but he was crying at the same time.

There was a sound upstairs; Beth getting out of bed. Coll edged closer to Louis. A moment later, the toilet flushed. Beth came out of her room and paused on the landing. Coll and Louis heard her walk into Louis's room and then come out and start down the stairs.

'Who the fuck's she going to be this time?' muttered Coll.

A moment later the kitchen door opened and Beth stood looking in at them. 'She was lovely, wasn't she, Louis?' she said. 'I had no idea. I was too small. And I came along and took her away from you and you never held it against me. You've always been so generous.'

She walked across, leaned over the table, and kissed her brother on the cheek.

Half an hour later, Beth was looking across the kitchen table at the frightened faces of her brother and her best friend, sitting safely on the other side of the table from her. She could hardly blame them. Even so, she felt oddly elated – triumphant, almost. Before, it had been a mystery. Now she knew — what had been going on, and why; and she knew what she had to do next. For the first time in days, there was hope.

'I'm the doorway,' she told them. 'There's something inside me that can pass from one world to another — from life, all the way down to death.'

'Like a medium?' asked Louis.

'More than that. That thing had to wait four hundred years for me to come along to get it out of its grave since it was last reburied. All that time. As soon as he found me, he must have known he could use me to escape. I've been fighting him off, but not just him. I was fighting Mum, too. Keeping her away. She knew what I was as soon as she died. It's like . . .' Beth struggled to explain what her mother had shown her. 'When your soul leaves your body you move into death — down into the darkness, where the dead gather. But after that, you move on somewhere else — into the light. Glory, she called it. Mum should have done that years ago, but she stayed behind for me. If Dad had let her, she would have protected me. But I was told to shut the door on all the dead, including her. And this creature — this thing, this demon or whatever — it found me and managed to push past Mum, push past me and use me to dig it up and set it free.'

'So you were possessed.'

'I think so. But now I know Mum's there I can let her in to help me. The demon is strong – stronger than me, and stronger than Mum, but not stronger than both of us together. Together we can keep him out. I'm safe. You see? He can't take me over any more. It won't happen again.'

Beth laughed with relief. To be able to go to sleep and not fear that she would kill her friends in the night! 'She's watching over me, just like in the fairy tales. That's what she said. Just like in the fairy tales.'

'Did she say anything about me?' asked Louis.

'She loved you, Louis, I knew that. But no, no message. She didn't have much time,' she added. Louis said nothing. Beth had no idea how much that pained him. Unlike her, he remembered his mother vividly, and how much it had hurt when she left for ever. Now she had come back – but not for him.

'What about Ivan?' asked Coll. 'Is he dead?'

Beth tried to remember what her mother had told her. 'Maybe, but maybe not,' she muttered. 'She said he hadn't arrived at death. That's all she knows.'

'So he's OK,' said Louis.

Beth frowned. 'I don't know. She had to go. She shouldn't really be in death any more, let alone here with the living. But I think – what happened to that thing . . . it's like a disease.'

'So it might be contagious,' said Coll. 'So Ivan might be diseased as well.'

'Maybe.'

'But he might be OK?' Louis pressed.

Beth nodded. It could be. Why not? You had to hope.

'So what's next?' asked Coll.

'We find it,' said Beth. 'We find it, and we kill it. It's as simple as that.'

666

'Finally.'

Ivan stirred and opened his eyes. He was frozen through in every joint, every bone, every muscle. He groaned and stretched.

'You are the first. Look at me. What are you?'

He turned to face the voice of his master. Thin hands groped weakly around his face. The master spat.

'The ghoul. Pathetic. It'll be nothing better than a dog in a month.' There was a long pause. 'Because it was already dead when I bit it. At least it turned. Can you understand me?'

Ivan nodded.

'Say "Yes."'

'Yeas.'

'It can hardly even talk. What's your name?'

He groped around in his brain for a name. His mind felt like mud. There were all sorts of bits and pieces floating around in it, but he had no idea what they had once stood for.

'I!' he exclaimed suddenly. It meant something. It was as close as he could get to a name.

'It knows it exists. Wonderful.'

'I,' he repeated again, in a disappointed kind of way. He had thought it meant more than that.

'Stand up,' the voice commanded. 'Let's have a look at you. Up, up. Stand!'

He pulled himself up to his feet. The master struck a flame from a cigarette lighter and regarded him. He looked fondly back down. His eyes filled with tears. He loved the master.

'Barely worth it. But all I have. When I am strong, I shall produce vampires, demons, gods. But for now I have you. Here to me, you bone cruncher.'

'I' shuffled forward. He tried to smile, but the muscles in his face were half paralysed.

Old habits die hard.

'You were going to go shopping for me. Instead, it will have to be theft. I shall have to come with you. Pick me up.'

He stooped and picked the lean figure up in his arms. He cradled his face against his. Love, love! Yes. 'I' knew love.

'Get back from my face, you idiot. You think I want kisses from a dog? Forward. Move. There are things we need.'

'I' shuffled forward. He was hungry. If he was good, maybe there would be food soon. Two thoughts rose in his mind: beer and meat. Beer and meat, meat and beer . . . 'Mmmm,' he drooled.

'Idiot! Keep your dribble off me!'

Averting his face to one side so as not to inconvenience the master, 'I' moved forward, out of the shadows of the derelict house and into the long night of his new life.

Chapter Nine

That night Beth slept deeply for the first time in a week. She awoke quietly the next morning and lay for a while in the dim light that came through the curtains. She felt that she had been on a long journey but that she was at last on her way back. She could trust her sleep. What a thing! Something that everyone else took for granted, and it was hers again.

She wasn't going mad. She wasn't a monster or a freak, nor a timid girl fighting mental illness, but someone with a rare and special gift. Now she was going to reclaim that gift for herself. She felt deep down inside herself, to the place where she had been scared to go for so long – and there it was, the link, coiling down to the twilight world where the dead assembled. Death was not a happy place, full of memories of dying, of pain, of regret and confusion.

Beyond it lay Glory, whatever that was – wherever it was; the true home of the soul. Her mother could have gone there, but instead she had stayed behind in these fields of pain and regret to help her daughter. All those years in the darkness, just for her. And this creature, the demon; this was where he lived. He had made his home right there in the shock and confusion of death, unable to pass on to the brightness that followed, forever trying to move backwards into the world of the living. How he must have rejoiced when he found Beth! He had seen his centuries of waiting draw to an end.

Downstairs she could hear Coll and Louis talking. Beth lay a little longer, enjoying the feeling of calm, unwilling to let the new day begin with all the fears and plans that she knew would go with it. But it was beginning already. Ivan was gone – but perhaps he could still be rescued. She pushed back the covers. She waited a few seconds longer, feeling the cool air on her for a moment, then swung her legs out of bed and stood up.

'For Ivan,' she thought. She pulled on her gown and went down to join the others in the kitchen, where they were discussing how to cover up Ivan's absence.

Coll looked dreadful. It wasn't surprising. About this time the day before she had been waking up next to a very cute boy in the secure knowledge that superstition was only for the ignorant. In a few short hours her entire world had been ruptured, blown apart, annihilated. So what else was true? God? The Little People? Father Christmas? The Ankle Grabber? She was doing her best to put on her usual bright act, but every time she thought about it, it made her feel sick.

In the night, she had crept to Louis for a cuddle. Nothing sexual – she'd hardly needed to say that. 'I'd go to Beth,' she said. 'But she doesn't feel safe any more, you know?'

Louis nodded and pulled the covers over her. He understood how she felt, but he had one big advantage over her in assimilating this stuff: he was a believer. This thing wasn't God – quite the opposite. But it fitted. Where there was light, there must be darkness. Somehow, on some level, it all made sense to him.

At least the business of what to do about Ivan was a simple, practical thing. He didn't go to lectures all that often but his absence would be noticed sooner or later. Should they inform the authorities themselves – or wait till someone else did?

They decided to wait a week before they did anything. Ivan had just wandered off without telling anyone before now. If they did anything too quickly it would only cause suspicion to fall on them.

'Maybe we can get him back,' said Beth.

'Back from the dead?' said Coll. 'Unless he's caught ghoulism, or whatever it is.' She shook her head as her stomach lurched inside her yet again.

Beth looked at her sympathetically. 'It does get more believable after you've lived with it for a bit, if that's any help.'

Coll nodded glumly. 'It's amazing what the human mind can adapt to,' she muttered. 'Just the fear to worry about, then.'

'Yep,' said Beth. 'That just keeps on hanging around.'

They had breakfast, made coffee, and got down to it. Coll had her notebook ready. 'Pluses and minuses,' she said briskly. 'Let's make a list, for starters, so we know where we stand. OK? We know it can turn into a hyena. Or do we?' she added hopefully. 'Maybe we just *think* we know it changed into a hyena.'

'Oh, please,' said Louis.

'It could be mass hypnosis. Ask yourself – which is the most likely?'

'Mass hypnosis,' said Beth. 'Unfortunately, in this case it's the unlikely we're dealing with. Write it down, Coll. It turns into a hyena.'

Coll wrote it down. 'I'd call that a minus,' she said.

'We know it eats human flesh,' said Louis.

'Minus.'

'And we know it'll kill to get it,' said Beth.

'Minus.'

'We know it can take over our Beth. Big minus,' said Coll, looking sideways at her friend.

'We know it can't now. Big plus,' said Beth.

'Not proven,' said Coll bluntly.

'Write it down,' said Louis. Coll did.

'We know it can survive for centuries in a grave, with no apparent ill effects,' said Louis.

'You can't say that,' Coll pointed out pedantically. 'I mean, it looked pretty run-down to me.'

'OK. It can survive in a grave for hundreds of years, maybe even thousands – but maybe it doesn't *like* it very much. OK?'

'Agreed.'

'What else?' asked Coll. 'That's a lot of minuses so far.'

'Our mother is helping us from the other side. Big plus,' said Beth.

Coll was doubtful about that, but she was out-voted. 'Dead mother helping out' got written down in the plus column. 'This is a psychiatrist's nightmare,' she sighed.

'And we know that a brick stuffed in its throat disables it,' insisted Beth.

'Better than that,' said Louis. 'We know how to kill

it – with fire. Two thousand years in a grave with a brick in its throat isn't enough for me. I want it so dead, it's never going to come back again.'

Coll looked uncomfortable. 'That may need verifying,' she said.

'You're not sure?'

'Come on, how can I be sure?'

'Just how reliable was that information you gave us?' Louis demanded.

Coll wavered. 'I might not have been taking this thing quite as seriously as I made out,' she admitted.

'Oh, great.'

'Maybe it can't be destroyed. Maybe it's immortal,' Beth said suddenly.

'You reckon?' asked Coll.

Beth shrugged. 'It was lying in that grave all that time, like Louis said – for centuries, maybe. No food, no water, no light. No air, maybe. But it didn't die. It just lay there, century after century, waiting. If it could be killed, whoever put it there in the first place would have done it then.'

There was a pause.

'That'll be another minus, then,' muttered Coll. They covered a few more possibilities then Coll ran them through the information she'd managed to pick up elsewhere. Ghouls appeared to have originated in Arabia, where they got their various names. 'Ghul,

Ghulah, Ghul of the waste, grave-creature, coffin-fiend,' she said. 'It's worth memorising them.'

'Why?' asked Louis.

'Some sources say you can combat supernatural beings by knowing their names,' Coll said. 'I know, I know, it sounds like crap, but hey, who knows? We should learn them just in case. There're Indian versions as well. Vetala, aka Baital, Baitala and Betail.'

'These are all the names of individual ghouls, right?'

'The Vetala are a race, apparently. A *Bhuta* is a woman who has died in childbirth, or been denied the correct burial rites when she dies. Some of this stuff stinks. It'll so suck if the supernatural world is even more sexist than this one.'

'It's not a her,' said Beth.

'Are you sure?' said Louis.

'She's right. The hyena had a dick,' pointed out Coll. 'I notice these things,' she added apologetically.

They ran through some more myths about ghouls, but they still had no way of knowing what was true and what wasn't. It was time for some serious research. Coll knew where to go. 'If there's one place where we can find out about this thing for real, it's the Collesbrooke Library,' she said. 'It was started four hundred years ago by Dr Dee. He knew a thing or two. There's a story that he summoned up the devil in his rooms in Manchester. You can still see the burn mark where he stood on the table.'

'Right. This thing of ours must be something to do with the Devil,' said Louis, with great certainty.

Coll shrugged. 'I'm an atheist, but what do I know? Anyway, the Collesbrooke is the real deal. If there's any genuinely useful information anywhere about this thing, it's going to be there.'

The Collesbrooke Library wasn't far away, in the small Cheshire town of the same name, about thirty miles outside Manchester. It took just over an hour to get there in Coll's Punto.

The town was better known for its four-hundred-year-old public school than for its library. In times past, the two had been closely associated and even shared staff. But although the school enjoyed the notoriety of having had magicians lecture for them in the past, it wasn't nearly so happy about having an active library of the supernatural so close to its doors in the present.

It was a pretty little town, on a river shaded by willow trees. You could hire boats and buy cream teas in the summer, but it was winter now, and the town was gearing up with pretty lights and displays to lure the shoppers in, off the narrow streets slippery with icy rain. The school was right in the middle of town, a picturesque jumble of red-brick houses, towers and chapels. The library too was right there on the main drag, in among the gift shops and cafes, but you'd never have noticed it unless you were looking for it. Beth, Coll and Louis walked past it several times before they spotted a window filled with remaindered stock – out-of-date cookbooks, out-of-copyright writers and glossy titles left over from last year for the tourist trade.

'That can't be it,' muttered Coll. But then they found two doorbells side by side on the door jamb, one marked bookshop, the other simply Collesbrooke.

'Here we go.' Coll rubbed her hands together. 'Maybe this ghoul-hunting has its upside after all. I'm going to enjoy this!' She pressed the bell. A few minutes later, an elderly man opened the door and beckoned them inside.

The librarian, Don Mayhew, was a shortish man in his eighties by the look of it, still good-looking despite the years. His office at the back of the shop was stacked high with books, and smelled of damp and old paper. He had white hair and was dressed in a pair of baggy old jeans and a creased grey shirt. He shuffled painfully as he led them inside, but was clearly delighted to see them. He made tea and produced a large plate of chocolate biscuits, which he watched them eat while he rolled himself a cigarette and smoked.

'Such a pleasure to see young people coming to use the library,' he said.

'Don't you get anyone from the school?' asked Coll.

'School doesn't really like us. There have been some scandals in the past, you see.'

'Yes, I read up,' she replied.

'Did you? Yes, a good few scandals. People take the supernatural far too seriously. Religious types, mainly. If you believe in God, there's not much reason not to believe in a whole load of other hocus-pocus as well, is there?'

'Don't you believe any of it?' asked Coll.

Mayhew waved his cigarette in the air. 'Oh, there's more in Heaven and Earth and all that, of course. But let's face it, most of it's just stories to scare the ignorant.'

That was disappointing.

'We're all believers,' said Beth.

'Nothing wrong with that,' said Mayhew stoutly. 'We get all sorts in here – Christians, Muslims, pagans, Odinists, Satanists. It's all the same to me,' he added. 'So. Tell me what exactly it is you're looking for in the library?'

'Ghouls,' said Coll. 'We want some information

about ghouls. Roman or Middle Eastern ones, preferably.'

'Ghouls.' The old man seemed a little disappointed. 'Well, you've come to the right place. The ghoul is Arabian in origin, I believe. They have a star named after them in Arabic. Ghoul, Ghul. Alghol.' He smiled. 'I'm sure you'll find what you're looking for. For a game, is it . . .?' he enquired tentatively. 'I get a lot of enquiries from people making computer games, or playing them. Ghouls seem to be very popular in gaming these days.'

'. . . not exactly a game,' said Beth.

'What can you tell us,' asked Coll, 'about "the hunger that never ends"?'

The old man looked at her sharply.

'Where did you hear that?' he asked.

'It was inscribed on an old brick we found,' said Coll. 'We're researching it. It was in Latin. "For the living, life; for the dead, the hunger that never ends."'

The old man sat still for a moment, thinking.

'A very good translation,' he said. 'And tell me,' he asked, leaning forward and picking up a biscuit, 'where exactly is this brick now?'

'At home,' said Beth.

'You didn't bring it. That's a pity. I would have liked to have seen it. Well, now, I think I have a book that may help get to the bottom of it. Hmm, who's the scholar? You, my dear — am I right?' Coll nodded and beamed. 'Good. You come with me — and Louis. Yes, I may need a hand. Beth, if you wouldn't mind running up to the library and fetching another book for us? It may also help shed some light on this brick of yours, and on any ghouls that may be associated with it.' He smiled sourly: ghouls were clearly a bit of a joke to him.

'No problem,' said Beth. They finished off their tea and biscuits and stood up.

'If you go out of this room and turn left at the door, you'll come to a staircase. Go up there and take the first door to your left. That will take you to the library. You'll find the book you want under P, for Mathew Pepper. It's called *The Undead*.'

'Did this guy Pepper have, you know, any direct experience?' Coll asked.

'Pepper claimed that his work was based on much older material, including some by our founder John Dee. It's his manuscript that I'm going to show you. Perhaps you've heard of him?'

'Wow. You bet. So he did some work on this stuff? I never knew.'

'Doctor Dee was a very inquisitive fellow, who got to learn a great deal more than was good for him,' said Mayhew. He laughed, throwing back his head, and looked suddenly and briefly young again. 'The book has a red spine, if I remember. Louis and Coll, if you'll follow me.'

As Beth made her way upstairs, Louis and Coll followed the librarian along a narrow, grubby corridor towards the back of the building and up a flight of stairs. There he ushered them into a room, full of boxes of books, old and new.

'One moment,' he said. 'I have to fetch something. I won't be a moment.'

Mayhew left the room and closed the door behind him. Coll went straight to the boxes and started rifling through them. Louis glanced at the door anxiously. 'Where's he gone?' he complained. 'I don't like leaving Beth on her own.'

Coll looked up from her box. 'That's a point,' she said – and, as she spoke, something approached the door to the room from outside. They could hear the boards creak, and its snorting breaths. It didn't sound much like the old man. Whoever this was, they weighed a ton. The door handle, a round knob, turned slightly but slipped back. And again, as if someone was trying to open it with slippery hands.

'Mr Mayhew?' asked Louis.

He was answered by a grunt. Then, someone – something – dropped down to the floor and started sniffing at the crack under the door.

'Shit!' Coll jumped up. Louis ran to the door and

flicked the catch on the lock, shutting them in. The thing on the other side gave a coughing growl and thumped on the door, a solid old oak thing set in a massive frame. There was a pause; then it pressed its weight against the, door which creaked and bulged slightly under the weight. Coll let out a little scream at the sight and was answered at once by a roar – there was no other way of describing it. The creature on the other side hurled itself against the door with such violence that the whole room shook. Louis leaped back.

'Shit!'

Then it spoke.

'Ledin,' it said. The voice sounded crooked and bent, like someone using the wrong throat to speak with, or as if they'd been taught by an animal to use words. It was also horribly familiar. Unconsciously, Louis and Coll retreated backwards across the room. The creature hurled itself at the door again. 'Ledin!' it bawled, and began tugging and heaving at the door handle, grunting and coughing with rage. Louis ran to the window and looked out. It opened up directly onto a narrow back street, some twenty feet below. There was no way out there – no pipes going down, no ledges they could move across.

They were trapped.

'Is it him, the librarian?' asked Coll.

'I don't think so. I think he might have gone after Beth,' Louis said. He stared at the door. The thing had stopped heaving at the handle and had started hurling itself at it again. With every blow the room shook. The door cracked and dust began to fall from the frame. At this rate it would be inside in minutes.

'We have to fight it,' Louis said.

'Are you joking? That thing is like the Hulk on steroids.'

'But what about Beth?'

There was another sickening crash as the thing threw itself once again at the door and bellowed in frustration and rage.

'God. OK. OK. Must think. Must think. Argh! OK. What have we got? Let's make a plan . . .'

Louis took off his rucksack and opened it. A chisel, various weapons . . .

'Rope,' said Coll. 'I'm good with knots. Used to be one of my hobbies. Let's trip him.'

She took out the length of rope that Louis had packed and tied it from the bottom of a bookcase on one side of the door to the leg of an armchair on the other. 'You go that side, I'll go this side. If it rushes in fast enough it'll go down. I'll try to get past it to get to Beth. You stab the fucker to death. OK?'

'It's a plan,' admitted Louis. 'Just not a very good

one. How about you open the door and we both leg it out?'

'It's a deal.'

'Ledin,' screamed the creature on the other side of the door. It hurled itself forward again. A cloud of dust rose up and bits of plaster fell to the floor.

'Ready?' asked Louis.

'No. But OK. Louis . . .'

'What?'

Coll turned, grabbed hold of him and kissed him hard on the lips.

'I've been wanting to do that since I was eleven. If we don't die, I want another one of those.'

'It's a deal.'

'Really?' she asked, surprised.

'Yeah.'

'Wow. Cool. OK . . .'

Coll looked at him over her shoulder. She shook her head; this was mad. Then she unlocked the door and flung it open.

The thing was on all fours, sniffing under the door. It was some kind of hideous cross between a huge ginger ape and a dog. It had a jaw like a shovel, a long, low sloping brow, and hugely muscled fore-arms which might once have been human. Its back legs were clearly half dog, half ape, and it seemed happier on its knuckles than on its two feet. It twisted its head sideways to look at them. Its eyes rolled, showing white.

'*Ivan?*' said Louis.

'I' charged.

666

The stairway led up to a dirty corridor which left Beth totally unprepared for the glory of the library itself. She opened the door to find herself standing at the threshold of a magnificent glass dome, flooding light down on to a quarter of an acre of bookshelves. Blinded, she paused and blinked. Something jumped up with a clap in front of her – a pigeon had somehow got in and was flapping around the upper shelves. There was nothing dark and secretive about this library, despite its subject. The shelves were arranged in concentric circles beneath the great glass cupola, with gaps to allow access from one ring to another, like a maze. Extraordinarily, as the sunlight streamed through from the glass above, areas of shelving steamed slightly. As she got closer, Beth could see why. The whole building was badly in need of repair and the rain had got in and wet the books. The thin winter sunshine, trapped under so much glass, was warming the books and causing vapour to rise.

The place was astonishing, but God only knew

how much damage was being done. If Coll saw it, she'd weep with rage. She couldn't bear to see books treated badly – especially books like this.

Beth located the alphabetical labels on the shelves and began her search. It didn't take her long – the red spine gave it away. *The Undead*, by Mathew Pepper, just as the librarian had said.

She took it out and began to leaf through.

The book was handwritten with just a few type-written pages, very blurry and badly done. She looked at the date in the front: 1821. The typed pages must have been done on one of the very first typewriters. No wonder the writer had given up – the quality of the print was so poor. But the book was in good condition. Fortunately, the rain hadn't found it yet.

She flicked through the section on ghouls and went straight to the bit she wanted – the part dealing with the ways in which they might be killed. Basically, this book agreed with the *Natural History of the Impossible*: burning was the only way. But it went on to add a warning.

'Care must be taken even when the body is turned to ash, for the ghoul may be easily mistaken for another, more dangerous creature of the night, the full demon. These beings have been known, in certain weakened conditions, to feast on human flesh and may be easily mistaken for their lesser cousins. But this monster may never be taken to its death, for it is truly immortal and its life may not be ended by any means we know.'

'Shit,' muttered Beth.

'By staking, or any other form of butchery, it may be thought that the monster is dead; but never having lived, it is unable to die. Upon being buried, the demon will claw its way underground like a mole to the neighbouring graves, to feed on the flesh of the corpses buried therein. It will partake of this food until it regains its strength and is able once more to resume its true nature, and take, first, human blood from a living person, and then, finally, to feast upon the soul itself.'

A demon! And it was growing! All the time, stronger and stronger. The longer they left it, the worse it would become.

'Although the true demon may never perish, it may be immobilised. A brick, blessed, made with holy water, and with an incantation imprinted on it, may be forced into its mouth to prevent its foul feasting. To this writer's certain knowledge, there are several thus interred, many in Italy, for it was the Romans who first learned of this trick, but over the rest of the world besides. At least two that we know of are buried here in England, one by this writer's own hand.'

'I can still taste that brick,' said a soft voice in her ear.

Beth froze. It was right behind her.

She turned slowly, as if she could avoid the strike by caution. It had crept up so silently on her that she had heard nothing and now it stood less than a metre from her: Donald Mayhew, the librarian himself. He stared at her with eyes like a reptile. 'I wake up at night tasting it,' he said. 'For most of the last two thousand years, it's been the only thing I did taste.' He shook his head. 'Did you imagine that I was stupid? An old enemy of mine founded this place. Of course, I came to make sure his book was safe.'

John Dee had founded the library. So the creature was telling the truth earlier when he'd said that Dee had written a book. The demon had given her a clue, if only she lived long enough to use it. It watched her now and laughed, guessing her thoughts.

'Beth! Do you think I would kill *you*, who released me, who brought me into the light? You cannot die. You belong be my side. You are like me. I promise, Beth — I will never harm you. I will only make you stronger, more beautiful. I will make you better.' He leaned towards her. But she was suddenly overcome by a stench — the stink of his soul, rotting for a thousand years or more.

She pulled back. He made a face at her revulsion.

'I am an old man, of course. But I'm getting younger every day. I shall be beautiful again soon. You can be beautiful with me.'

Beth stepped back. 'Coll and Louis?' she asked.

'Downstairs. An old friend of yours is keeping them company,' he said. And he smiled.

Ivan. So it was true; the disease was infectious. Beth began calmly rummaging in her handbag, as if she was looking for something she needed. She was – a weapon. The demon watched her curiously. She pulled out a cross.

'I'm not a believer myself,' he said. He laughed, showing the spiked fangs at the front of his mouth that he used to pierce the skin, and at the back, fat molars to crunch up bone. He smiled again. 'It's lucky you came. I have Dee's book. Now I know where the brick is. In this age of disbelief, who else is there to challenge me? I cannot be stopped.' He stretched out his arms in a sudden burst of joy. The sunlight fell on his face and he closed his eyes for a moment, enjoying the warmth. 'I have been in the dark for so long. To be young again. To feel the sun on my face. I am at the threshold of great things. I will have you, Beth!' He stretched out a hand, but she shoved him in the chest so he staggered back. He hissed in anger. 'Don't make me bite you now. You would become a poor thing, like your friend. You want that?'

'Ivan. Where is he?'

'He has become a ghoul. But that's not for you. I need to taste you when I am at the height of my strength. Beth! Listen. I offer you everlasting life. All the riches of the world. Beauty, wealth, eternity! Beyond this life there is no God, in case you were wondering; only the grave. Everlasting hunger, darkness and eternal misery. How can you say no?'

'Let my brother and my friend go,' she croaked.

The creature smiled. 'It's too late for that, I suspect. Your boyfriend's hunger is as great as mine.' He stretched out a hand towards her cheek. 'You could learn to love me,' he crooned. 'Love is not hard. You just have to decide. You are the channel, I am the power. Together, we will rule the two worlds. You cannot say no to me.'

So he wasn't going to kill her. That gave her a chance to kill him. 'You're not selling it to me,' she said; and, as calmly as she could, dug in her bag for another weapon.

Suddenly his hand shot out and he seized hold of her. 'Look – here – into my soul. See what is waiting for you if you say no.'

He seized her head in his hands and gazed into her eyes. Inexorably, like a leaf on the edge of a vortex, Beth felt herself, spinning, spinning, deep into the black hole of the demon's mind . . .

666

'I' knew he had seen both the people in front of him before, but he had no idea if they had ever meant anything to him. The name Ivan, too, felt familiar — it rang some distant memory, but he did not associate it with himself; his name was 'I', and Fool, and Ghoul now. And anyway, none of this counted against his desire to crush them for his master and — above all — to feed. His hunger was immense. No matter how much he ate, it never diminished.

He came rushing in at them like an avalanche, tripped over the rope and fell headlong into the room, breaking the fall with his chin and very nearly biting his tongue in half. Blood flooded his mouth. Briefly stunned, and confused with pain, he was aware of something slipping past him and swung out at it. His claws caught on the cloth of Coll's top, but she tore free and ran out. He turned to pursue her but again got caught on that rope. He bellowed with rage, hunger and the dreadful fear of what his master would do to him if he let them go. Then a staggering pain shot through his lower body. It was such a devastating ache that he fell to the floor and clutched at himself, curling up into a foetal position and letting out an odd, whistling groan. Louis had used Coll's trick and kicked him in the balls. He'd landed it just right. Ivan was momentarily disabled.

Seeing his chance to end it, Louis ran to him, knelt by his side and raised the big woodworking chisel from his bag high in the air. Beneath him, Ivan gaped and rolled his eye. He saw his life ending and gasped. 'Don' kill,' he begged.

Louis paused.

'Do it! It's not him any more!' yelled Coll. But Louis, staring at the remains of his friend's face, was not ready to strike.

'Ivan!' he hissed. 'Look at me! It's Louis.'

'Louis . . .' repeated the beast.

'Kill him or he'll kill you,' screamed Coll. But Louis was unsure. Ivan grinned cunningly and swatted at him, knocking him away. Coll screamed – but Louis had tumbled to the door. Ivan was squirming over onto his front as Louis rolled out of the room. Coll ran back, slammed the door shut as Ivan hurled himself at them.

'You idiot,' yelled Coll.

'Let's go!' Louis shouted. Together they ran for the stairway. They hadn't reached the stairs when there was the sound of splintering wood behind them and a roar like a lion's. Ivan was breaking down the door.

✻

Upstairs, Beth gasped as the demon released her.

'You see?' he begged. 'An eternity of loneliness and hunger. It awaits us all. But you and I, Beth . . . together we can outrun death.'

Beth staggered back. The demon had showed her a darkness so black, a hunger so deep, that nothing could ever satisfy it. This was what awaited her, this was what lay on the other side of life; this was death. The misery of it took her breath away.

'They all lie,' said the demon sadly. 'The God-lovers, the rationalists, the superstitious. Life is short and sweet, and death is bitter and long. There is no end to consciousness in the grave. There is not one of us who wouldn't swap eternity for a few seconds longer in the sun. I can give you joy forever.'

Beth was breathless with the misery of it. It was all so bleak, so inevitable – and the demon was offering her escape. But inside her there was another voice, calling her name: her mother, fighting with her, forcing back the power of the old man's greed. And in the darkness with which he had filled her mind, a whisper, a thread, a frond of light. There was another place beyond death . . .

'You're lying,' Beth hissed. She forced herself back to the safe shores of the world she knew – the here and now, the light all around her, the books, the ground under her feet. Her hand was still in her bag and she closed her fingers on a weapon – a short chisel she had taken from her dad's workbox. 'With you? Not even a choice.' She lunged before she had finished, but the old man dodged her and caught her wrists. Together they struggled but, old though he was, his strength was inhuman. He bent her hand back so that she yelped, dropped the chisel and sank to her knees.

'Don't force me,' he gasped. His lips parted and he bared his fangs.

'You're a vampire,' she said stupidly.

'Nothing as easy as that.' He bent, and licked the exposed skin on her neck, dribbling on her in his greed. Beth heaved at him but he wouldn't budge.

'Not yet, darling. Not yet,' he crooned. He convulsed, and flung her away from him with a sudden burst of superhuman strength. He sank his hands on his knees and panted. 'Another few days,' he gasped. 'When you see me young, then you will know what glory is. You will not be able to say no. Then I will bite you. We will spend eternity together.'

From somewhere in the building, something banged violently. Whatever it was, it was so powerful that even up here, the floor quivered.

The demon smiled. 'Your boyfriend sounds annoyed.'

But then there was another sound – feet running

towards them. He straightened up. 'Idiot!' he hissed. 'I will burn him for this.'

Louis and Coll were on the stairs. Beth made to run, but the demon caught her by the arm. The door to the library burst open.

'Beth!' bawled Louis. She filled her lungs to answer, but the demon clamped his hand over her mouth and began to drag her backwards. She heaved against his grip and tried to shout, managing only to make groaning sounds in her throat. At once he caught her by the neck and squeezed.

'You will be silent,' he whispered in her ear. But Louis and Coll had already heard her. They began to run, seeking her out, but the shelves were arranged like the walls of a maze and there was no clear path towards her. One of them – Coll, she thought – ran right past her, no more than a metre or so away. Beth was tugging at his fingers around her neck, but the darkness was closing in on her as he cut off her air and her blood. As hard as she could she hurled her weight sideways against the shelving. A section came crashing down, making a deafening noise echoing under the glass dome above them. At once, Coll was there. She flung herself at the demon and helped Beth force his fingers away from her neck. Then Louis arrived, chisel in his hand, up in the air ready to stab. He didn't hesitate this time, but flung himself at the old man, hacking down at him. The creature batted at the weapon and its sharp edge ripped the cloth of his jacket, skidding and bouncing on his ribs as it came down.

The demon elbowed Beth and Coll away and ran, but Coll grabbed hold of his arm as he passed and spun him round. 'He's weakening,' cried Beth. It was true. The demon was still old, his strength was limited. They had him!

Louis tackled him around his legs and he fell to the ground. Together they wrestled him, the old man spitting and cursing them – a dreadful sound, in several voices and languages at the same time. Beth snatched up the chisel. She managed to twist round and stab at his chest, hard, with one hand. The old man cried out in pain but the chisel skidded off his sternum and failed to penetrate.

There was a terrifying brief struggle, in which all three of them fumbled desperately at his throat, at his eyes. Then, suddenly, they had him down, Louis lying across him, Beth and Coll sitting on his legs.

'The chisel,' gasped Louis hoarsely. But it was out of reach.

Stalemate. All three of them lay there, panting.

'For you,' the gasping creature hissed at Louis, 'there is only death. But for your sister there can be everlasting life, and eternal joy. Let me go and I will give her the world!'

Louis tried to reach for his throat, but he snapped his teeth, just missing his hand.

'Don't let him bite you. He'll – like Ivan,' warned Beth.

As if in answer, a rash of fur sprang up on the creature's face, his face bulged forward, his arms moved to the front.

'He's changing – quick!' Coll yelled. There was another fumbling fight as they adapted to the new shape, holding the great dog down, pinning its head. It was strong, stronger than the man he'd been; but it was still weakening and they were still its match. They got it back down again, and this time Louis managed to grab the chisel. He handed it to Coll.

'Right on the heart!' he demanded.

Coll stabbed the chisel down and held it in place. The demon cried out in pain. Louis grabbed a thick book that had spilled onto the floor and slammed it down on the tool's handle. A blossom of blood appeared in among the fur. The creature screamed, a thin, high screech. The chisel remained upright in his chest, partially embedded in bone.

'Again!' hissed Coll.

Louis pounded down – One! Two! Three! Each time the creature screamed; but each time the book bounced back and he failed to fully penetrate the bone. With a violent tug he pulled the chisel out and smacked it down a few inches lower, avoiding the sternum. This time the chisel sank into the flesh. Coll steadied it. Again, Louis whacked it with the book. This time it dug in deeper, but still not deep enough. Louis struck again, as hard as he could, and again! Again! Again! But still the chisel would not go through.

'What the fuck!' Louis cried. What did he have to do? Then, behind them, the door burst open again. There was a roar, and a rattling of claws. The bookshelves literally burst apart – and there was Ivan. He seemed to have grown to twice his previous size in his rage. He howled and roared and pawed the ground, the eyes in his head rolling in fury.

They fell back at once. Enraged, Ivan leaped forward and attacked the first thing he saw, which happened to be a bookshelf. He ripped it to pieces, and, in a bound, launched himself at Beth, knocked her down and bending his head, spilling saliva into her face, sniffed at her.

'Ivan,' she begged. 'It's me. It's Beth! Don't you know me? Remember, Ivan! Remember me?'

The beast paused, as if surprised, and looked down at her, drool still dripping from his jaws. He shook his head. Beth reached up to touch his face.

'Ivan,' she whispered. 'Look at you. Oh, look at you, Ivan. What has he done to you?'

Ivan stopped moving, still growling deep in his throat. Then he frowned; he could still move the muscles on his face like man – but only just.

'. . . Eth,' he said. His mouth and throat were no longer made for speech, but he was trying. 'Eth . . .?'

'Beth. Remember,' she begged.

For a moment Beth thought he knew her. But then he squealed as his master banged his muzzle onto his throat. Ivan turned and crouched low. The demon let him lick his hyena lips for a second, and then the two beasts ran together up the aisles to the door, the demon leaving a trail of blood behind him and swaying as he ran. They had been so close to finishing him, so close! There was a moment while one of them batted at the door, trying to open it, then they rushed out onto the stairwell. There was the sound of clawed feet rattling on the boards as the beasts ran downstairs; and then they were gone.

Chapter Ten

They lay on the floor, surrounded by a litter of books. Below them a door banged. The demon had escaped again.

'Everyone OK?' asked Beth.

'I couldn't do it,' panted Louis, almost in tears.

'It's not your fault, Luey,' said Beth.

'But what's the use?' he raged. 'We had him. We'll never get another chance like that.'

'We will get another chance,' said Coll. She crawled across and put her arms around him. 'You were great, Louis. That bastard must be even tougher than we thought.'

'You were really whacking that chisel,' said Beth. 'I can't believe you didn't get through.'

Louis shook his head in despair. He'd failed at the only important thing he'd ever had to do in his life.

Coll hugged him hard, pressing her face against his, but she felt something wet. She pulled away. There was blood on him.

'Your neck's bleeding,' she said. Louis slapped his hand to the place, but there was no wound. They had to search, and eventually they found blood on Coll's sleeve. When she rolled it up, there it was — a wide, curved row of indentations where one of them had bitten her, and two puncture marks on her forearm close to the wrist. She stared in disbelief.

'I never felt a thing. It doesn't even hurt.'

'Which one was it?'

'He bit me. He bloody bit me.'

'It looks too small to have been Ivan,' said Louis, examining the wound. 'Let's get it washed.' He stood up and held out his hand.

Coll pressed her fingers into the wound. 'I can't feel it. Must be some sort of anaesthetic. Shit. I thought we'd got away with it. Shit.' Her face crumpled. 'I'm not going to end up like that.' She looked up at Louis. 'Don't let me end up like that.'

'Hurry, though,' said Beth. 'Wash it.'

Louis pulled her up and they ran downstairs to the bathroom by the office. Coll filled the sink with water and splashed her arm, trying to rinse the punctures out as much as she could. Then she sucked at it and spat the blood out. Two minutes later it was still bleeding steadily.

'Anti-coagulant,' Coll said. 'He must have got every sort of shit into me.' She glanced up at them. 'Don't look so glum,' she said. 'Maybe I can work from the inside. Double agent, you know?'

'It doesn't mean that,' said Louis.

'It could mean a whole lot of things,' said Coll. 'And death isn't by any means the least attractive.'

'It's only a little bite,' said Louis. 'It had to go through cloth and we washed it pretty quick. It doesn't mean—'

'You know what?' said Beth suddenly. 'We have to get back home. We told him the brick is at home – he wants it.'

'But that's great!' Louis was jubilant. 'It means we get another chance. Come on!' He made to leave, but Beth held him back.

'Hold it, hold it. There's more. He said something else – a book by John Dee.'

'That's important,' said Coll.

'We don't have time,' said Louis. 'If he gets that brick we've had it.'

'We have the car and he's on foot,' said Coll. 'What if the Dee book tells us how to kill him? We have to find it.' Coll and Beth headed off to begin the search. Louis, furious at the delay, followed them. They started in the office, and for once they struck lucky. They found it almost at once, wrapped up in an old polythene bag on the desk. On the spine was the title: *The Diary of John Dee.*

'This has to be it!' she crowed. She opened it up. Handwritten. It was going to take some deciphering. They'd spent only a few minutes and Louis was anxious to leave at once, but Coll wanted to search for more books.

'We can't wait!' insisted Louis.

'Don't panic.' Coll started shuffling through the other material on the desk. She'd found a couple more books that she thought the creature might have been reading when they were interrupted by a scream from the bathroom. Beth. They rushed through . . . But it wasn't the monster. She had discovered a body lying in the shower; it had been there the whole time, while they talked, while Coll had been washing her arm. It was a man, tall, well built, in his forties, with brown hair going grey at the sides and a gingery beard. He was as pale as a ghost, and a substantial part of his lower torso had been devoured.

It was the librarian, the real Don Mayhew. What was left of his body was unnaturally pale. Louis bent down cautiously, tilted his neck to one side and found a wound there about the size of a fifty-pence piece.

'Like a vampire, now,' said Coll.

'OK,' said Louis. 'Now we go.'

666

Coll continued to bleed all the way home. Worse, as they approached Manchester, she started to get drowsy, to the point where she had to pull over and let Louis take the wheel. Beth kept asking her how she felt, and Coll's answers were getting shorter and shorter and more and more blurred. Physically she looked just the same as ever, but Beth remembered how it had been with her. They might not know Coll had changed until it was too late.

By the time they arrived at the house she was still conscious and even tried to get out with them to help. But her legs gave way under her as soon as she tried to stand.

'Lumps of lard.' Coll clapped her hand to her arm and looked suddenly stricken. Her eyes filled with tears. 'Sorry . . .' she began. Beth turned and hugged her.

Louis put a clumsy hand on her shoulder. 'You won't turn, you won't turn,' he said.

'If I do,' said Coll, 'You deal with me, OK? Promise.'

'We won't have to.'

'No. Promise. Right now, before you even go in there.'

Louis nodded. 'I promise.'

'Me, too,' said Beth.

Coll nodded, turned and went back into the car. 'Go on,' she told them. 'See if it's there. I'll wait here.'

They could smell him as soon as they opened the door – a rank, strong smell of wet dog and decay. He was upstairs, ransacking the place. They ran up, Louis first. The demon was in Beth's room, standing there in human form as the old man, going through the drawers. Ivan was sitting on the bed, his huge head almost level with the light shade. He turned as they came in, curling his lips and growling a warning. Stay back!

It was the first time they had seen him properly. He looked huge, sitting on that bed. His shovel jaw, still with a recognisable chin, the sparse hair on his flanks, the curiously bald cheeks and, above all, the eyes made him look horribly human. Their friend was still in there somewhere. He got down on all fours as they came closer, and crouched, ready to leap, the fur on his spine rising up in a thick dark line all along his back.

At the same time the old man began to change, but

it was apparent that he was now very tired and very weak. The fight, and getting here so fast, had told on him. He could hardly stand, and even as he sank to the ground and began the turn, he staggered on all four legs and lurched against the wardrobe. Even so, he was enormous, his shoulders reaching up above the chest of drawers. For a few seconds, they could see a human face imprinted on his muzzle. Then it was gone.

The demon lowered its head and growled, a deep snarl that they could feel vibrating through the floorboards. Suddenly the room stank even worse, an overpowering stench of rotting flesh.

'It's not here,' Beth said. 'We've hidden it where you'll never find it.'

'The next time you see it, that brick is going back in your mouth for eternity, I promise you that much,' said Louis.

He bent to draw the chisel out of his bag. At the same moment, Ivan launched himself into the air straight at them. They flung themselves aside, but Louis twisted as he did, and managed to strike him in the shoulder . . . a long ragged wound that raked down onto his leg. As Louis crashed to the floor, Ivan bawled in pain – 'Yah!' – in a human voice. The hyena ran past, barging Beth to one side, charging out of the door and down the stairs. Ivan followed, moving backwards to keep his face to them, snarling and growling, snapping up at them with his huge jaws, keeping them back while his master made his escape. As they edged down after them. Louis lunged with his chisel, trying to land another blow. Beth had picked up one of her shoes from the floor on the threshold and lobbed it at him, but he just snapped at it and kept to his task. He was going to remain between them and his master at all costs.

Once again, Beth tried to get through to him.

'Ivan,' she called.

The beast paused to glance at her, but then looked over his shoulder at the demon, afraid of betraying him.

'Don't you know me, Ivan? It's Beth.'

The creature that had been Ivan made a whining call.

'He's crying,' said Louis. 'Don't stop.'

'Ivan and Beth,' she said. 'Remember? It sounds good, huh? You and me, Ivan. How about it?'

Ivan whined again, and produced a terrifying and fearful expression on his face – a wide baring of his teeth, a furrowing of his brow, his lips turning up at the corners. They had no idea if it was a smile, a grimace, a snarl or all three. Further up the hall the demon was already scrabbling at the front door. He got a paw behind it and pulled, but his other foot was in the way. He glanced behind and whimpered – the first sign of fear they'd seen. He tried again to wrench the door open. This time he succeeded, staggered outside, and called – that dreadful, snickering yell. Ivan turned, leaped down the remaining stairs and out the door after him in a smooth, powerful movement Louis and Beth close behind him. Outside, both beasts had paused by the car with Coll in it. Ivan was standing by the vehicle's side, staring straight in; the demon himself was on the bonnet, clawing and mouthing at the glass as if he could bite his way through it. Inside, Coll was screaming hysterically.

Louis yelled and hurled the chisel at it, but missed. The demon cast them a savage look, jumped down off the bonnet and loped off up the road. Ivan cast Beth a final, lingering glance, and followed on. They were round the corner and gone in less than a minute.

Again! They were as far from finishing him off as ever.

Beth and Louis ran up to the car. The windscreen was covered in slobber, where the creature had been literally drooling to get at Coll. Inside, her face as white as ash, Coll was still screaming.

They tried to calm her down as they helped her out of the car and into the house. Coll was on fire now, burning up with a fever, her legs buckling under

her. Between them they lugged her inside, sat her at
the kitchen table and got her to drink some water.
Gradually she grew quieter. Together they got her
upstairs, and Beth hustled Louis out while she got her
friend undressed.

'Louis,' called Coll as he left. He turned to look at
her. White face, scared black eyes.

'I'll come and tuck you in later,' he said.

'Great – I have to get turned into practically
another species before he'll even look at me,' Coll
said. She smiled at Beth, and fell suddenly asleep.

Beth didn't go down to Louis at once, but sat on the
bed for a while in the sudden stillness, just sitting,
trying not to think or feel anything. It had been a
maniacal ride, getting faster and stranger all the time,
full of danger, with discovery after discovery – about
herself and about the world around her. Somehow,
despite the fear and disorientation, she was taking it
all in and going forward, still trying, still undefeated.
But now it looked as if they were two down. It was
impossible, wasn't it? What were they thinking? No
one could defeat this thing!

Coll had been right there with her the whole time,
so brave, so loyal. She could have left at any point, but
hadn't. She'd never even mentioned running away. If

she turned against them, it would be a devastating blow.

'I'm like a disease,' Beth thought. But there was more at stake than just herself or her friends. She knew in her heart that it wasn't her who was the disease – it was the creature they were hunting. It wasn't even about loyalty to each other – it was about loyalty to humankind, to life. Stopping just wasn't an option. They had to carry on, even if it cost them their souls. But – what if it meant actually having to kill Coll? Could she do that? She wasn't sure she could.

Reluctantly, Beth got up and left the quiet of the sickroom to find Louis in the kitchen, drinking juice from a carton.

'Want some?'

'Go on, then.'

He handed her the container. She took a swig and asked him outright. 'Will you do it?'

Louis rubbed his face. 'You've seen how good I am at killing,' he said.

'Louis, don't leave it up to me,' she said. 'Please don't.'

There was a pause.

'Have we made up our minds already?' he asked.

'We made Coll a promise,' said Beth.

'The point is,' said Louis, 'can we keep it?' He

glanced at Beth and looked away, fearful of meeting her eyes. 'It's not come to that yet,' he said.

'But if it does. Say yes, Louis.'

Louis stared at the window. There was a phrase in his mind. It had been in his mind ever since the idea had arisen that he might have to end a life. 'Thou shalt not kill.' The commandment was so much a part of him. With the demon it was bad enough. How would he cope when it came to doing it to a friend?

'I'll try,' he said. 'But you know what, Beth? I can't promise. I just can't.'

Beth nodded. She swigged back some more juice. Maybe it would be up to her, after all.

'I love you, Louis,' she said.

'Love you too, sis.'

'You could have gone, but you never did. I'm so lucky.'

Louis sighed. 'Yeah,' he said, and laughed. 'Lucky doesn't seem to quite say it, does it?' They came together for a hug, then he sighed. 'OK,' he said. 'On with the show. We'd better start packing.'

'Why?'

'He knows we're here, doesn't he? He could be back any time. We have to get out.'

Beth sagged with exhaustion. She'd thought they were going to get a break, if only for the night, but it wasn't going to happen. She glanced outside at the darkness gathering in the garden. Louis was right. Where was the demon now? How far away was he? How near?

'It's not going to end, is it?' she said. 'Not for a minute.'

'Not until we're dead or he's back in the ground,' Louis said.

'But where do we go? Not home. We can't take it to Dad, can we?'

'I don't know yet. Let's think about it while we get ready.'

'And what about Coll?' she asked.

Louis shook his head. 'She can't come with us,' he said. 'Not until we're sure she's clear. In the meantime, keep something sharp on you,' he added. 'And — fingers crossed.'

Packing didn't take long — they didn't need much. The tricky bit was trying to remove any clues that might lead the demon to them or to their parents. Anything with their home address on it — letters, university admin and so on — all had to go. It took hours. They hadn't realised till they tried to wipe the tracks away how traceable they were.

They packed the brick and the book, ready to go with them, flung their stuff into bin bags and did the same for Coll. Upstairs, like a human time bomb, she slept through it all. It was nine o'clock at night before she emerged. They heard her using the toilet and went to find her in her room, but not before they'd concealed kitchen knives in their pockets. Coll looked pale but otherwise normal, as far as they could tell. Ivan had changed physically so they took it as a good sign that she hadn't, and chatted a bit until they decided that she was, almost certainly, still herself. Louis told her they were planning on going into hiding.

Still drowsy, Coll nodded. 'Where to?' she asked. When no one answered, she frowned and thought about it. 'Am I coming? I mean . . .?'

Beth winced. 'If we tell you and you turn, you'll know where we are.'

'Right. Jesus,' said Coll, and shook her head. So — she was on her own.

'Sorry, babe,' said Beth. 'What can we do?'

'Nothing. Stay alive. That's all.' She nodded. It was hard. She understood, but she looked stricken. They had to leave her behind.

'I'm really sorry, Coll, I'm so sorry,' said Louis. He felt dreadful. Like Beth, he had been impressed at how totally she'd been there for them — and here they were already deserting her. 'How are you feeling now? OK?'

'Better. I felt really strange for a while, but I feel just fine now. A bit dopey still, that's all.'

'Maybe it was just shock,' said Beth. 'Maybe you fought it off.'

'Maybe.' Coll gave them a half-smile. 'Body fluids can be so nice in the right circumstances. Wrong time, wrong place.'

'Wrong person,' agreed Beth. 'Tell me,' she asked suddenly. 'How do we know if it's you or if it's not you?'

Coll looked back at her, unsmiling. 'I guess we won't know the answer to that,' she said, 'until it's too late. Same as us with you, sweetie, eh?'

They had worked out a place to go. A friend of their dad's, an old client of his who had become a personal friend, owned a static caravan near Whitby. She was always telling them they could borrow it whenever they wanted to. They could pick up the key from her in Hebden Bridge, just down the road from where their dad lived, and go straight there.

Louis wanted to go now – that night, that minute. The demon was gaining strength almost by the hour. They'd already rung the owner. She'd been surprised. Really? The caravan? In the middle of winter? And they wanted to pick it up now? It'd be two in the morning by the time they got there. But she was willing. She wouldn't stay up, but she'd leave the key under a stone by the back door.

They could go any time.

'We have to duplicate the book first,' Coll told them. 'There's just one copy in existence. Even if we only live long enough to do that, it'll be worth it. At least the knowledge will be out there for someone else. Anyway, wherever you're going – how are you getting there at this time of night?' she asked.

Somehow, without thinking it through, they'd both assumed they'd be going with Coll in her car.

Coll smiled. 'You're on the train. And you're going to have to wait till tomorrow morning. Guys, it's gonna be a long night.'

'You could lend us the car,' said Louis.

Coll paused. 'One more night,' she said. 'That won't hurt. I'm not ready. Please.'

'We stay with her,' said Beth. 'Look at her. She's just the same. It's Coll.'

'We don't know,' insisted Louis. He paused, wanting to stay but scared. He peered anxiously at Coll's face.

She put on her best winsome smile. 'Promise I won't bite,' she said.

Despite himself, Louis laughed. 'It looks like you,'

he conceded. 'One more night. But we can't stay here, can we?'

'Agreed.' Coll whooped and ran over to kiss him. 'Thanks, Louis.'

Typically, Coll had a plan B – a set of keys to the house of a friend who had already left for Christmas and had given Coll the keys so she could pop in and water her beloved house plants. No one else would know they were there. It seemed safe. They loaded up Coll's Punto and left at about one in the morning. The demon, or Ivan, might be watching even now, so they went a long way round, right out onto the M56, around town and back in the other side.

Beth sat in the back and watched the city lights and the dark shapes of the night rush past. The house in Fallowfield had been such an adventure when she'd moved in, just a few months ago. Her first place away from home. Now it was a relief to get away, but it wasn't any kind of break, not while Coll was in danger. They would have to wait for the caravan in Whitby before they could really relax.

Beth closed her eyes and leaned back. She was exhausted – they all were. They made jokes about how rough they looked as they drove along – black rings around the eyes, faces gone a greenish white, and their sweat smelling acrid, like cat's pee: the smell of fear.

'Showers all round. Beer. Pizza,' said Louis. They all cheered. Such little things – such stupid things – but they sounded so good. No wonder, thought Beth, that the dead were clamouring to get back to life.

Really? she thought. Pizza. Is that what it's all about? 'There is not one of us who wouldn't swap eternity for a few seconds longer in the sun,' the demon had told her.

'No pizza in the grave,' she said out loud. Coll leaned over from the front seat to smile at her as the car revved up onto the motorway and sped away around the city, and the rain began drumming hard on the windscreen.

Coll's friend Sall's house was bigger than theirs. Six people lived there, but everyone except Sall had locked their doors, so they only had the use of one bedroom, the kitchen and the sitting room. Not that they needed more space – they had no intention of sleeping that night. With Coll the way she was, it was just too big a risk. Tomorrow there would be sleep. Tonight there were still things to do.

They had their showers, ate some pizza, and got on with it. The first thing they had to do was scan the pages of Dee's book. Coll took her scanner with her, along with her laptop to do the job. They emailed each of themselves a copy and saved it on a number of different servers, so that whatever information was in there stood no chance of ever being lost again.

Now they just had to read it – and that was going to prove far harder than duplicating it. Not only was Dee's handwriting dreadful, he had used several different languages, all of them, of course, archaic. Slowly, they worked their way through the opening pages, which at least were in English. In them, Dee claimed to have released a genuine demon from the grave, which he had, after a tremendous loss of life, managed to put back in the ground on English soil, in Manchester, fifty years later. By the morning they had managed to build up a better picture of what they were up against.

According to Dr Dee, the monster he had released was already several thousand years old by the time he'd encountered him. The Egyptians knew of him; so did the Greeks. He appeared again in Roman times, where he had made his way right to the heart of government, the Senate, before he was tracked down and interred in what was modern-day Syria.

He had appeared again in the eighth century among the Arabs, who had given him his current name, and, as he had told them himself, named a star after him. They had eventually reinterred him in the grave he had escaped from, using the same brick that the Romans had used — the same brick, in fact, which Dee had put back in the monster's mouth with his own hand, centuries later.

His name was Alghol.

The demon, Dee claimed, was like an insect: his life history took him through several different forms before he finally achieved his true self. Dee confirmed what Pepper had said, that the cycle began from death. After apparent burial, the demon awoke and burrowed through the earth like a grub. Still too weak to attack the living, he confined his attention at this early stage to the dead. In his weakened state, it might take him weeks, months or even years to reach another grave where he could feast on the flesh of his fellow corpses. Once he was able to feed, however, he developed at an astonishing speed.

Soon, when he had regained enough strength to rise out of the grave, Alghol turned to the living to satisfy his hunger, drinking their blood. But even this was not the end of the story. In his final form he did not simply feed on the body; he fed upon the souls of the victims. And this was the most dreadful thing of all, because unlike mortal death, which lasted only a short while before the soul moved on, the death that Alghol brought about lasted for ever. The victims were enslaved. Their strength became his, their life force at his service, trapped in the realm of death for eternity.

There it was. They had a name: Alghol. They knew his history. He had been released before and reburied many times thoughout his long life. It had been done before; it could be done again. There was hope.

And there was more hope promised. Dee claimed to know how to actually make the bricks that could be used to immobilise not only Alghol himself but the other demons, ghouls and vampires that he might spawn. These bricks could immobilise the monster and his brood, and freeze them to the darkness and hunger underground. And more: Dee hinted at another technique that could finish the demon for ever, that could actually end his life and send him back to where he belonged, all the way to Hell.

Hell – just the place for Alghol. But how? Dee claimed to have written everything down, but did not say where. It could be in the same book, of course, hidden in another language. So far they hadn't even worked out what all the languages he used were. But they could not tell for sure. Dee could have concealed it anywhere.

Meanwhile he confirmed what they had already

seen. The demon got not only stronger but younger with every day that passed, every bite of flesh, every sip of blood and every soul he swallowed. In the short time that he had been out of the ground, he had already turned from dust and bones to a vigorous old man. Judging by the wound they had found on the librarian's neck, and the corpse's pallor, he was already drinking human blood. Less than two weeks had passed. Would it be days or weeks before he was feeding not on flesh, not on blood, but on the human soul? Then his victims wouldn't simply pass on, or turn into another form of life. They would die for ever.

If they were going to finish this, they were going to have to do it soon.

'Nothing about how we can bring his victims back, though,' said Beth.

Coll shook her head. So far, the only way out was an eternity underground with a brick in your mouth. Not good. She didn't even want to think about it.

They got back to the book, but by five a.m. they were too tired to carry on. They broke open the beer, heated up more pizza, drank a toast to Ivan, and tried to relax. Coll was still feeling good. The demon had no idea where they were. Beth's mother was standing guard over her — why not? They watched a movie to pass the next few hours — one of the *Bourne* films. By halfway through, Coll found Louis snuggling up to her on the sofa. She glanced across to Beth and put on a surprised face. Finally!

'Louis, are you actually showing an interest in me?'

'I might be.'

'What's brought this on?'

'Just getting to know you, I suppose.'

A thought struck her. 'Is this pity sex?' she demanded.

Louis blushed. 'It's not even sex, yet,' he said, which made her laugh.

'You want some vampire kisses? Is that it? Look?' Coll opened her mouth and showed him her teeth. 'No fangs. You want to wait till I get some fangs?

'No fangs is fine. Even better, really. I don't want anything getting pricked.'

'Oh! You forward boy!'

Beth sighed. 'I hate to say this to you guys,' she said, 'and I know it's none of my business, but you know it's infectious, don't you?'

'I know!' said Louis. 'I'm just . . . lining things up for later.'

Coll laughed ruefully. 'Just my luck. I've been trying to get you to bed for years and as soon as you say yes, I get the worst STD in history. Not even any

kisses,' she said, holding up a finger as he got closer.
She smiled. 'Wow. Saying no. It's kinda fun, isn't it?
I'm on a promise, though, huh?'

'Yep.'

'Good. All I have to do now is stay alive.'

Chapter Eleven

Coll dropped Louis and Beth off at the station a couple of hours later. She passed over the goodbyes as fast as she could, ignoring Beth's tears and Louis's awkward attempts to express his feelings.

'Now we're getting on with it,' she told them. 'And we're going to finish this fucker off.'

She felt positive this morning. Finally they knew what they were up against and what they were doing. She had obviously reacted to the bite, but had fought it off. She was strong; they all were. Between them they would see an end to this thing. The only fly in the ointment was the beginnings of a toothache – the outcome, she supposed, of all the sweets she liked to suck while she was studying.

After leaving her friends, she drove straight to the university. She had some work to do there before she decided on her next move. She was wondering if Alghol would seek her out to see if his bite had captured her. Ivan's body had gone an hour or less after he had been killed. Was that him seeking his master, or had his master come for him? Maybe there was some way she could lure the demon to her. All she would have to do then was work out a way to finish him off. The muscles on his chest and belly were like armour. But there had to be a way into him somehow.

The work at university didn't take long, she was done by mid-morning. The toothache was getting worse, though, and in an act of rebellion against her own mouth she ate a whole Snickers bar for lunch. A brain like hers needed those calories.

An hour later her jaw was hammering.

The pain was difficult to locate — it seemed to be pulsing all across her upper jaw. She went to the loo to have a good look at herself. She looked OK. A bit puffy, maybe. She felt her jaw. Was it swollen?

All those sweets.

As she stood there, she realised it wasn't just her teeth. Her whole face was sore, and so was her neck. She had a headache coming on and the skin on her thighs and tummy felt sore to the touch. 'Period?' she thought. But the times were all wrong.

'Flu. Ovulation? Please.' she muttered. Something

she ate? Undecided, she stood staring at herself in the mirror. She looked odd. There were some nasty bugs going around. Loads of her friends had similar symptoms.

Suddenly she'd had enough. OK, she admitted it – she was going down with something, but she didn't yet know what it was. She had no intention whatsoever of turning into any kind of ghoul, vampire or demon, and she knew exactly how she was going to deal with the situation if it arose. Meanwhile, she needed some good old-fashioned spoiling. She left at once and went to her car. Maybe it was flu, maybe it wasn't. Either way, when she wanted nursing her instinct was the same – head for home. No one ever looks after you like your mum.

666

At about the time Coll was arriving at university, three men called round to the house in Fallowfield. One of them, a shortish, older man with iron-grey hair and a deeply lined face, stood back while another, a taller, younger man, pushed a wheelchair up the path towards the door. The occupant of the wheelchair was concealed by a blanket over his head that left his face in deep shadow. At the door, the younger man put his fingers to the lock and pushed, his body leaning slightly back against the pressure he was exerting. The door groaned and burst suddenly open. The man levered the wheelchair over the threshold and pushed the occupant inside. The older man followed and closed the door behind them. Inside he kicked irritably at the wheelchair.

'Ghoul. You wouldn't fool a cat. Out and seek. You know what we're here for.'

Ivan crept out of the wheelchair, head lowered submissively.

'Seek. Book, brick. Beth,' he added hopefully.

'Beth is mine. If you turn her into one of you, I'll nail you to a rock. Fool, it can't be trusted for a moment. Go with him,' he ordered the other man. 'Restrain it from eating the furniture. Don't forget, it is no longer able to read.'

'Yes, General.' The tall man followed Ivan up the stairs, where they began tearing the rooms apart. Downstairs, the demon Alghol wandered around, sniffing for scent, opening the cupboards, looking through them for clues.

Passing a mirror he caught sight of himself and spat. His weakness disgusted him, but in fact it was already passing. With every hour his glory returned. He had lost decades since he'd last met his enemies. He was on the threshold of youth, entering into the dominion of his power when he would feed not on the corporeal, on the living flesh, but on the eternal, on the god in us all, the soul itself. This time he would be greater than ever. This time there was Beth. He had known as soon as he felt her living presence, her brightness, penetrating his misery, down into the grave itself, that she was a light in the darkness, a beacon leading directly from death to life and back again. Hers was a gift unlike any other. Once he had devoured her and made her soul a part of his, her gift would be his as well. He would be able to move through the two worlds, feeding not only on the souls of the living, but on those of the dead, as they passed through the darkness from this world to the next.

And the next world on from there – the place of light on the other side of death itself, where pure soul dwelt? Glory was its name. Long, long ago, his own ambition and greed had twisted him so utterly out of shape that he was debarred from approaching it, trapped for ever in the realms of life and death. One day, though, when he was strong enough, he would burst out and take that world too, wherever and whatever it was. That was his aim – to destroy the light; to devour eternity itself.

The book and the brick – he needed those. But he wanted Beth most of all. She was the first step on the way. Once he had taken her, nothing, not the brick, nor any power or prayer or blessing or curse, would be able to keep him in the grave any more. Freedom to feed, freedom to grow. He was on the threshold of eternal power.

The tall man came downstairs to report. 'General, forgive me. they've gone.'

'I know.' Irritably, Alghol made his way up the stairs. He prowled around restlessly while Ivan sat on the floor of the room that had once been his, mouthing something held between his paws.

'They took everything,' said the tall man. 'This was the only room that had anything in it.'

'What's this?' Alghol bent and took the thing that Ivan was mouthing. A phone.

'It must be his. Sorry, General . . .'

'Two fools. Two idiots. There may be clues on it.'

'General – sorry! But look – I found this.' The man took a laptop from the desk. 'Ivan's, too, I think.'

'Show me.' Alghol sat down on the bed. The tall man joined him and fired up the laptop while Alghol checked the phone.

'Coll is on here. A home address. Good. She will lead us to them. You can fetch her for me, if you think you can handle it,' he told the tall man, who flushed with pleasure at the trust that his master was placing in him.

Together they began to scan through Ivan's messages and emails. Ivan himself lay unhappily on the floor at their feet. He wanted his phone back, even though he had no idea what it was any more. He was missing his friends, he was missing his beer, he was missing his life. Most of all though, he was disappointed because he kept letting his master down. He would do anything he could to put that right.

Coll arrived home at about 11:30 a.m., starving hungry. She had a cup of tea, a huge bowl of cereal and about half a loaf of bread before texting her mum to say she was home, and going to her bed, which lay made and ready for her as always. She was awoken an hour or so later by a text from Beth.

'How's it going?'

'I've gone to Mum's. My face hurts,' she texted back irritably. She rolled over and tried to sleep some more, but the fear gnawing at her insides prevented her. After a while she realised it wasn't just fear; it was hunger. Despite the cereal, she was ravenous.

It was a bad sign. Coll refused to give in to it and, after tossing and turning for what seemed like hours, fell into a restless sleep.

She woke up some time later, being stroked. She opened her eyes and stared at her mum for a moment, remembering what had happened to her. Then she turned over and groaned.

'You all right, darling? What is it?'

'Ill,' groaned Coll.

'And you've come home to be nursed! I'm so flattered!'

Coll turned over and stared at her mother again, trying to test if she wanted to hug her or drink her blood and take a bite out of her. To her relief, the hug won hands down. She sat up and wrapped her arms around her.

'I feel dreadful,' she confessed tearfully.

Her mother put a hand on her forehead. 'You have a temperature. Bed rest and a course of intensive spoiling for you, I'm afraid.'

'I'm starving,' said Coll.

'Lunch coming up. What do you want?'

'Fry-up?' said Coll hopefully.

Her mother expressed surprise. A fry-up wasn't the sort of thing her weight-conscious daughter usually went for. Coll was feeling unusually meaty today.

Soon the smell of bacon and egg came wafting up the stairs. It drove Coll to despair, and she knocked on the floor and begged for cereal for starters. She ate her food guiltily and greedily, and finished the lot off with two cups of tea, an apple, and an extra slice of toast and marmalade. At the end of it she felt sick.

'I'm not surprised.' Her mother shook her head, bemused, and left to get back to work. She'd run home from the town centre, where she worked as a lawyer, to see her beloved daughter at home.

I shouldn't be here, thought Coll. If she turned, she might kill her mum and her brother, who was at school at that moment. She glanced anxiously over at her bag lying by her bedside. Inside was a small bottle full of a yellowish liquid; her escape clause. She had prepared it in the university labs earlier that morning. She had no intention of eating dead people, or drinking their blood, or of spending eternity in a box. Nor was she going to trust Beth and Louis to do the job for her. If she was going to go, she was going to go by her own hand.

The thing was to get it done before she turned – but not too soon. But how could she tell? The hunger was a bad sign, a very bad sign, but was it enough evidence for her to kill herself right now? She was still herself. Surely there was still a chance.

First off, Coll took a look at her blood under the microscope – her room still housed bits and pieces from the many hobbies that she had taken up during her school years. It looked OK, but she was no blood expert. She got on her laptop and pulled up some images of human, hyena and wolf blood. Result! Hers was nothing like that of the beasts.

Not yet. Perhaps not at all. She still had time, and she was going to use it for some focused research. The brick had gone with Beth and Louis, but she had her copy of Dee's book and the original, which she was planning to do some tests on. She'd look through that. The history was interesting, but so far they hadn't found anything that was going to be actually useful. There must be something more, hidden among the pages. Why else had the demon been so keen to get it?

Coll called up a Latin dictionary online and began the laborious work of picking her way through the text.

The inevitable call from Beth came an hour later.

'You OK?'

'Tiny temperature,' said Coll. 'Mum's being hysterical about it. Ever since she did that first-aid course she thinks everything I get is some sort of mortal illness.'

'Better take some aspirin,' said Beth, which made Coll giggle. Immediately after, without preamble, she started to cry.

'Don't,' said Beth.

'I'm not,' lied Coll. 'I'm not only too young to die, I'm too gorgeous. It would be a tragic loss to Man.'

'You mean men, don't you?'

'Yeah. All of them. How's Louis?'

'He's right here.' Beth paused. 'Do you want us to come over?' she asked carefully.

'No! I don't want anyone to see me, especially him. I look like some kind of badly cooked pudding.'

'Right.' There was another pause, while Coll realised that wasn't what she'd meant.

'If I need – if I need to be dead, I have the means here,' she said.

Beth couldn't help it; her first thought was relief that she wasn't going to have to do it herself. 'Just sit tight,' she said. 'You sound good to me. We don't want to lose you, baby.'

'Even if I turn?'

'Even if you turn,' replied Beth.

'That's a nice thing to say,' said Coll. 'Even if it isn't true.'

'Louis wants a word,' Beth said.

The phone rustled and Louis came on the line.

'Hi.'

'Hi. Doesn't look like I'm going to make girlfriend after all, does it?'

'I'll be waiting,' he said. Then – 'I'm praying for you,' he added.

There was a pause.

'Symptoms?' he asked.

Coll hesitated. She didn't want to admit it. 'Toothache,' she said. 'And hungry. That's not good, is it?'

'How hungry?'

'Pretty much all the time,' she admitted.

'Feed a fever, isn't that what they say?' said Louis.

'You think?'

'Yeah. It'll be OK . . .'

'Don't talk me round, Louis. You really don't want me in denial, you know?'

'Right,' said Louis. He paused a moment. 'You don't want us to . . .'

'You'll make a mess of it,' said Coll. 'You're too nice. I wouldn't trust you to step on a beetle. I have poison with me. OK?'

There was a shocked pause on the other end of the line.

'Right, I'm going now,' she said hurriedly. 'I'm . . . speak later, OK?'

She put down the phone abruptly. She waited a moment to settle herself before leaning over to her bag and taking out the little bottle. She looked at it fearfully. She hadn't realised up until now, when she was about to lose it, how much – how very, very much – she loved being alive.

Louis turned off the phone and handed it back to Beth. They were on the platform at York station, waiting for the next leg of their journey to Whitby.

He kept telling himself that they'd done the right thing but it felt all wrong, just leaving Coll to her fate like this. They were in it together, weren't they? Then shouldn't they stay together?

In his heart he knew there was no choice, but it was eating him up. After all these years, she'd finally found a way into his heart, and within days he was losing her. There had to be something they could do.

'She's going to kill herself,' he said.

'I know. Did she say when?'

'I don't know. Soon, I think.' Louis looked at the pale oval face of his sister. 'We have to help her.'

'Yeah, but how?'

'Mum. She can help us, can't she?'

'Mum?' Beth was amazed that he could ask. She grimaced. 'Louis, I feel just like you do. But it doesn't work like that.'

'Well, how *does* it work?'

'I don't know how it works.'

'But you talked to her once,' said Louis furiously. 'She's inside you. You've got to get her to help us, Beth.'

'I don't know how! You don't know what you're asking . . .'

'Just ask her!' he hissed. He looked round and dropped his voice. People were watching. 'She's come all this way for you. She's been there all these years for you. She can do just one thing for me, too, can't she? You ask her. You tell her. We need to help Coll.'

He turned and left abruptly. Beth stared after him. Something for him? Was that how he saw it?

'She comes when she comes, that's all,' she muttered to herself.

The train wasn't due for another half an hour or so. Beth went to the toilets and locked herself in one of the cubicles to try and pull herself together. She didn't need to pee but went through the motions anyway, and sat there staring at the door, wondering what to do.

Louis was right, she had to do everything she could to play her part. But asking the dead for favours? She didn't understand why or how, but it felt profoundly, deeply wrong. The idea of seeking her mother out just didn't add up. Inside her was that passage that lead down to the realms of death, but she had never travelled it herself. Now Louis was asking her to do just that.

The idea filled her with horror. It was as if he was asking her to die.

Beth pulled up her jeans and went out to wash her hands. Someone else was standing there already, touching up her make-up. A couple of other women came in and went to the cubicles, chattering away.

Beth studied her face in the mirrors above the sinks. A plumpish figure looked back from dark-rimmed eyes. A pale oval face, dark hair. A faint moustache on her lip. Coll was always nagging her to wax. It was time for that again. Not at all like Louis, who was tall, with light brown hair, taking after her father. She was her mother's daughter, all right.

She looked into her eyes. How deep did they go, what lay behind them? More than just flesh and blood, apparently. The dead could use something hidden in her to travel back to life. Was it possible for her to travel back to them? To follow her gift back all the way to its dark roots where her mother stood silent guard against demons in the darkness?

And if she did, how would she get back?

Her mind recoiled. Louis didn't know what he was asking her!

She looked again. Behind her eyes, the world slipped away. The woman by her side left, and another came out from behind her to wash her hands and straighten her face but Beth saw none of it. The world yawed, heaved, and then stood still. A minute, an hour, a day. She lost all track or even meaning of time.

'Are you all right? Excuse me? Are you OK?' the woman by her side asked her. Beth did not respond. She was staring into a place that no man or woman could ever know from this side of the grave – a world of seamless darkness, of hunger, of rage, of aching desire. And it was populated, too. Beyond the darkness she could hear the yammering of the lost dead – of the souls stolen to feed Alghol's greed and ambition.

From behind her in the mirror – but really it was within her, she understood – a haggard face appeared over her shoulder. Her mother? It was a death's head, but that didn't mean anything. The head paused, jaws agape, staring at her. And behind her, in the darkness, another face and another, and another. Beth saw the true horror: the legions of lost souls, the nameless army – the hideous dead.

'Get out! Go, Beth, go!' someone screamed.

Bang! And the vision was gone. Beth fell backwards onto the floor and lay still.

'Are you all right?' Distantly, Beth heard the echoes of a voice. It dawned on her that something was wrong, but she wasn't sure what it was. Everything was very still and quiet and gentle. She opened her mouth to speak and realised that she had stopped breathing. Her heart was still, too. That's odd, she thought, and in the silence that followed she realised that she was dead.

Dead? That was wrong, surely? She tried to sit up, and suddenly her jaws opened and she sucked in air.

The sounds of the station came rushing in, the woman's voice, footsteps on the tiled floor as more women came to see what the matter was. Then, with a rush of blood, her heart restarted. Beth sat up, gasping and coughing. So many lost souls! She felt sick to her core. She had travelled to the realm of death, and she had almost died doing it. What did she expect? Thank God she hadn't been on her own.

'Are you OK?' the woman asked again. She held out her hand. Beth took hold of it and pulled herself to her feet. She put her hands to her face. Warm blood, a beating heart. She had made it back in time.

'Thanks,' she said, and walked rapidly away.

With no car it was an awkward journey to Whitby. They'd had to go to Hebden to pick up the key, then catch the train to York, then to Darlington, then to Middlesbrough. It took the best part of five hours, including a taxi at the other end. It was gone three by the time they arrived.

Beth had never really got caravan parks. Row after row of boxes, all neatly laid out like tombstones. It was freezing cold and the field was sodden after days of rain, but inside the caravan it was surprisingly spacious and comfy. There was a great view – not from the caravan itself, but if you went outside you could see across the cliffs and over the sea, iron-grey and frosted with white horses in the wind. Best of all, no one knew they were there. This was as safe as they were likely to get.

Louis turned on the gas and the water, while Beth unpacked the stores they had bought in Whitby and made a meal – fish fingers and oven chips. He came back in and grinned at her. She smiled back cautiously.

'We're on holiday,' he said in a surprised voice.

'It's going to drive us mad,' Beth pointed out.

'It'll be fun,' he insisted.

'What are we going to do?'

'Play games. Read. Go for walks. Traditional things.'

'Sit in the caravan and look at the rain. Bicker,' she said. They always used to bicker on holiday.

'We should have brought the Monopoly,' said Louis.

'Good we didn't,' she said. That was the thing that always caused the most arguments. 'We can build sandcastles while the grown-ups have a nice rest,' she added.

'We are the grown-ups,' Louis reminded her.

Beth nodded and smiled grimly. 'Yeah. I bet Dad never had to deal with this sort of shit, though.'

Louis looked out the window.

'Let's go into town after dinner,' he said. 'Buy a book. Horror story, maybe. Didn't Dracula stay in Whitby at some point?'

'We already have a horror book to read,' said Beth. 'Written by Dr Dee.' She came over to serve the fish fingers.

'Cheer up,' said Louis. 'It might never happen.' And, despite herself, Beth laughed.

They did the holiday thing. Ate their fish fingers and chips, washed up, then went to explore the little town, walked on the stony beach and tried to find fossils. Beth wanted to sleep when they got back, but Louis was still feeling restless, so he left her to have a doze while he went out to walk the sea cliffs. It was half past three, already getting dark, but there was still a little light in the sky, shining on the sea, which seemed to glow slightly in the twilight.

It was beautiful walking along the cliffs, but Louis's mood was low. He'd been trying to be bright for Beth, but on his own he let himself go and felt his heart fall inside him. What chance did they stand? One by one they were falling. Only Beth was safe, with their mother standing in the Kingdom of the Dead, guarding her. He loved the idea of his mother doing that. But he missed her. He'd been missing her for fourteen years. She'd been with Beth the whole time, and he just wished she could have spent some time with him as well.

And Coll. And Ivan. What kind of situation was it where all you could do for your friends was kill them? God help them.

Louis paused. He'd barely had any time for God in the past day or two. Stupid! – forgetting your best hope. He bent his head there and then, and clasped his hands together.

'Help us, oh Lord. Help us, Mother.'

He paused. What was he saying? It wasn't Mary he was addressing, but his own mother. What the hell, he thought – but at least he was certain that his mother was there.

Louis stood in the wind, overlooking the sea, and struggled to find a connection with God inside him. He didn't get far. Even with his eyes closed, he had a sense of something flashing in the sky around him, a bright light slicing through the darkness. He opened his eyes and was amazed to see beams of light, like lasers, cutting up the sky. He turned; it was the caravan. Even at this distance it was so bright, it hurt his eyes – beams of light firing out of the windows, lighting up the night, even the clouds above. He hadn't heard a thing. It was all happening in utter silence, like a scene from a film with the volume turned down.

'Beth!' he yelled, and he ran to help her.

666

Coll read and read and read, but found nothing. Maybe it was the wrong book after all. Her brother came home from school, and chatted a while, but she was beginning to feel weird again so she claimed sickness and sent him away.

She dozed a while, and woke up to the smell of cooking. She went to take a look at herself in the mirror. Her skin was pale and waxy – corpse-like was the phrase that came to mind. The soreness in her skin had spread over her stomach and up her chest. Her breasts and her face were both tender to the touch.

'But what use are symptoms when you don't know the disease?' she asked herself. She checked her pulse. Her heart was beating away as usual, slow but strong. 'Not dead, that's a start,' she muttered. Finally, she bared her teeth at herself in the mirror – and there it was. The front four teeth in her upper jaw had grown longer and sharpened. She stared at them for a moment in disbelief. The toothache. Of course. But – so quick! She must be going through calcium like a cow. She ran her tongue across them, then touched one with the tip of a finger.

Ouch.

Coll went back to her bedroom, sat on the edge of the bed and wept. That was it, then. The other stuff, that was all the usual sort of thing. Sickness, diarrhoea. You got those things with gastric flu, with food poisoning, all sorts. But not teeth.

She picked up the small bottle of yellow liquid, which she had hidden under her pillow. It was bitter, quick and fatal. Carefully, she unscrewed the top and held it up to the light.

'Just another teenage suicide,' she whispered. '"We had no idea there was anything wrong," her mother said. "She seemed so happy. She even had a new boyfriend,"'

Her mother. This was going to destroy her family – and she couldn't even tell them why. The thought was unbearable. Was now the time? Her face was changing but she still had her own mind. Did she dare wait? She paused, undecided, but her mind was made up for her by the sound of her mother coming upstairs. Hurriedly, she screwed the top back on the bottle, stuffed it under her pillow and dived back into bed.

Her mother knocked at the door and entered, bearing dinner – a plate of shepherd's pie and peas. 'How's my hungry girl?' she wanted to know.

Coll smiled, trying not to flash her fangs, pulled

herself upright, and allowed her mum to put the tray on her lap. She felt like bursting into tears. This was goodbye, if only her mother knew it. She was also hungry – desperately hungry. Her last meal; shepherd's pie. Could be worse. Why not? Life goes on, she thought – or not, as the case may be. She picked up her fork and got stuck in. As she ate, her mum was watching her closely. 'What's the matter?' Coll snapped.

'You look odd,' her mother said. 'How are you feeling?'

'Better,' said Coll, keeping her upper lip clamped firmly over her front teeth.

'What's wrong with your mouth . . .?' began her mother, but stopped suddenly when she caught sight of her daughter's hands.

'My God, what have you done to your fingernails?' she demanded. Coll looked at them. They had grown. The nails were rolling in on themselves. There was no doubt about it – they were turning into claws.

'Nothing! Just a game – something for uni. A play. *Buffy the Vampire Slayer*. I'm a vampire,' she said unhappily.

'Well, take them off, they look disgusting,' insisted her mother.

'I can't. I'm practising. I have to eat with them on in the play,' said Coll. 'Teeth, too, see,' she said, and bared her fangs for her mum to see. If you're lying, Coll always thought, carry it through.

'Gross,' her mother told her. Coll sighed. Lying to her mum was so easy. Sometimes she wished she'd see through it and catch her out. So far, it had never happened.

She had to finish the food with her mum sitting on the edge of the bed staring suspiciously at her. It tasted funny: thin and muddy – unsatisfying. Her hunger returned violently as soon as she had finished eating, but she said nothing.

As soon as her mother left the room, Coll got up and looked again in the mirror. The teeth were rather sexy, in an odd way, she thought. Her fingernails were turning into sharp little talons – neat, pointy, and razor sharp, as she found out when she pricked the palm of her hand.

'Skin-piercing devices,' she thought. Truly, she was turning into something else. She opened her mouth and stuck her tongue out . . . and it just went on coming – crawling out of her mouth, inch after inch. What on Earth was that for? Lapping up blood, maybe? Carnivores as a whole had long tongues, she realised. That was what she was – a carnivore.

The tongue was disgusting. She didn't even want to put it back in her mouth.

Coll felt under her pillow, took the bottle out and unscrewed the top. Carefully, she tipped the contents into the glass of lemon barley water that her mother had left by her bed. She picked up the glass. Now was the time.

Coll was ready to die. But she wasn't ready to die in vain. There was one more thing to do. She put the bottle down and picked up her laptop. A goodbye to Beth and Louis, a list of her symptoms, a quick summary of what she had gathered from the book over the past few hours. It wasn't much to leave behind but it was all she had.

'Ten minutes,' she promised herself. 'And then it's time to die.'

She began to type.

It was only a hundred yards or so back from the cliffs, but Louis kept getting blinded by the beams of light shooting out of the windows of the caravan and out of the cracks under the door – blinding white, so intense that they might have come from the sun, turning the caravan into something like a star.

He ran up and pushed the door open.

Beth was hovering in mid-air at an angle of about

forty-five degrees, a metre off the ground. The light was coming out of her — from her eyes, from her mouth, from the tips of her fingers, from the fronds of her hair. It was so bright he could only watch in brief glances. It felt as if it would burn out his eyes.

'Beth, stop it!' he yelled.

His sister turned her head to him. Her eyes were terrible — like wet grey stones shining. She opened her mouth and out of it came a terrible vomit of noise, a cacophony, a babble of shouting, screaming, yelling, cursing, hissing, begging voices. The sound of it, the level of it, made Louis's hair stand on end. He tried to force himself towards her, but his body simply refused to approach her in the grip of sheer physical fear.

It had to be the demon. He edged his way round the chaos floating in the centre of the carvan to the cutlery drawer and took out the longest, sharpest knife he could find. To kill his own sister . . .? If he had to, yes. But he needed to be sure . . .

For another second the terrible apparition hung, flaring, screaming and gibbering in front of him. Then it stopped abruptly. Beth fell like a stone, banging her head on the floor. Louis's fear vanished at once at seeing her injured, and he ran forward and took her in his arms.

'Beth,' he begged. He held his breath in case she answered in another voice.

'I'm back,' she gasped. 'I'm OK, Louis. OK. It's me.'

'Who was it? Him?'

Beth's eyes looked up at him, bewildered. 'No! Not him. Mother . . .'

'Our mother? *That* was our mother?'

'Not just her . . .'

'Well, what? What was it?'

Beth lay, panting with shock and exhaustion. She tried to sit up. 'Ow!' She put her hand behind her head. She had a bump coming up as big as an egg.

Louis helped her to the table and sat her down. 'What was it?' he asked again.

'Don't know.' She sat there panting, trying to find her voice. 'I tried to find her, but I got lost among the dead. She was there somewhere, though.' She paused, gulping for air. Louis waited for her to go on. 'She was trying to show me something. That light. Glory. Then she had to leave. But the voices. All those people. Louis – I think that was for you.'

Louis stared down at her. He had so, so much wanted something from his dead mother. Was that it? Her offering for him? The screaming of the dead?

'And Coll?' he begged.

Beth closed her eyes for a moment, and sighed.

'Nothing,' she said. 'Sorry, Louis. She's on her own.'

There was a noise in Coll's room. She sat up with a gasp. She'd been asleep again. A figure stood there, at the foot of her bed, looking down at her. A man. She'd seen him before — but where? Then she remembered. It was Donald Mayhew, the librarian from the Collesbrooke Library. The last time she'd seen him, he'd been dead.

He looked much better alive.

Coll shrank back in the bed. Mayhew stepped round the bed, leaned over, took her by the upper arms and pulled her up as if she weighed no more than a feather. Gently, but with an irresistible force, he took the top of her head in one hand and held it still, as if in a vice. With the other hand he forced a finger into her mouth. Furiously, Coll bit down as hard as she could.

Mayhew shook his head and smiled. His fangs, Coll noticed, were well developed; no doubt now about what he was. He waited a moment until she relaxed, before running his finger around under her front teeth.

'Alghol will be disappointed,' he said. 'We had hoped you would be — ah, joining us. Instead, you're going to have to die.' In surprise Coll ran her tongue over the teeth. They were flat. No points, no extra length. Had she just imagined it? She looked at her hands; her fingers had returned to normal. There was the empty bottle of poison by her bed; there was the lemon barley water, undrunk. Could she have imagined it so clearly that she'd nearly poisoned herself for no reason?

'Guess I had a lucky escape, eh?' she said.

'No, Colette. You've actually been very *unlucky*,' he told her. 'To be bitten by Alghol – to have even a fraction of his gifts passed on to you – that would be lucky. Most die. I am lucky. I have become something like him – not entirely, of course; there's only one Alghol. But I will live for hundreds of years. Strength, power and wealth. I shall see things and go places you can never dream of. You missed out, Colette. You could have had all this. Instead, it looks as if you went and developed immunity. You'd have been dead by now otherwise. He said this might happen. You took only enough of his saliva to inoculate yourself. Now, that's what I'd call bad luck. We were hoping I might be able to bring back a clever and attractive companion. Instead . . .' He shrugged and pulled a sympathetic face.

'Instead, you're going to spend a long time in a hole with a brick in your mouth, what's so great about that?' Coll replied.

The vampire regarded her coolly. 'I think you'll find that very soon there'll be no one alive who knows how to do that any more. But I am keen to get this over with, so let's make a deal, shall we? You *are* going to die, Colette. Make up your mind about that. That's all there is to it. But there is the matter of what happens in the next hour or so leading up to your sad demise. I could, for example, torture you. Not very nice. I could feed you to your friend, Ivan. Painful as well as ironic. I could perhaps lead up to that by feeding your mother to him in front of you, so that you die knowing you could have prevented her death.

'That's one path. Another is – you tell me where the book is, and you tell me where the brick is. Then you can go quickly. I'll drink your blood – bingo! It's at an end. Your mother lives. You don't have to spend your last moments begging me to finish you off. And I don't get to ruin this rather nice carpet you have down.'

'Sod you,' said Coll shakily. 'Sod you, mister.'

The vampire smiled at her, and touched the tip of his tooth with his long, rough tongue. He leaned down to the pile of books that Coll had at her bedside. 'What have we here?' He picked up John Dee's book.

'It's all written down on the computer. Emails to everyone,' said Coll. But Mayhew wasn't bothered. He opened the book and bent the covers until the spine split.

Coll winced. She couldn't bear to see books badly treated.

The vampire peered into the back of the book. From the broken spine he pulled out a stiff, folded sheet of old parchment. He opened it up and glanced through it.

'Here we are. Written by Dr Dee himself, and hidden here by one of my predecessors at the library many years ago – just in case the wrong person got their hands on it.' He smiled and patted the page of manuscript. 'Too late.' He slid it into his pocket. 'That's one. Now – the brick. I need the brick, Colette.'

'I'll take the screaming and begging, thanks,' said Coll, although she knew she wouldn't, not when it came down to it. Pain had never been her good point. The vampire smiled. 'It can be arranged,' he said. He stood up. Coll glanced over at the bedside cabinet, where the glass of lemon barley water stood, out of reach, along with the little bottle of poison. She'd been stupid – delayed too long! Could she reach it in time?

Mayhew's gaze followed hers. 'What's this?' He picked up the little bottle and sniffed it. He glanced at her, then touched his tongue to it, and spat.

'Yeah. Too late. Thought I'd save you the trouble.

I'll give you a clue about the brick, though,' said Coll. 'It's not under the bed. So fuck you, dog-mouth.'

Mayhew shook his head and frowned; the poison was not nice. He wiped his mouth on the back of his sleeve, and then reached down to take a gulp of lemon barley water, to rinse the taste away. He paused. He liked it. Then he lifted it to his mouth and swallowed it all down.

'Wow,' said Coll. 'You know what? That was a seriously bad move you just did there.'

The vampire took a step towards her. A look of surprise crossed his face. Coll jumped out of bed and scuttled back across the room. The creature made to follow her – and crashed to the floor.

'Silly me,' said Coll. 'I have to admit I didn't fancy taking it down neat, so I put it in the barley water. Sorry. I guess I lied.'

The vampire stared up at her from the floor and hissed like a snake.

'Wow.' Coll was shaking. She ran her tongue over her teeth again. Immunity! They'd had bad luck for so long. Finally something good was happening.

'You thought you were going to drink my blood? Well, now you're dying, and I hope it hurts. And you know what? After I've read that piece of parchment you've got in your pocket, I'm gonna do the same thing to your boss, too. So much for hundreds of years of life and power, eh? You didn't even make one, you numpty.'

Mayhew quivered and lay still. Coll put her face into her hands and sobbed, but only briefly. She waited a moment for her nerves to settle before getting up and cautiously taking his pulse. It was still there, banging slowly away.

'Another few minutes at the most,' she thought.

Five minutes later, Mayhew's pulse was still beating – slower, perhaps, but Coll wasn't sure what that meant. For all she knew, vampire's hearts might beat slower anyway.

'There was enough in there to kill a horse,' she muttered to herself. She paused, unsure of what to do. The signs were that he wasn't going to die at all. She was stuck with a vampire in her bedroom, and he was waking up. She had to finish him off, quick. It wasn't going to be easy. There was a lot of information about crosses, holy water, garlic and other stuff – but the one thing everyone agreed on was the stake through the heart. While he was out, she could do it – if she could pierce his skin. The only trouble was, she didn't seem to have any stakes handy. And it would be pretty messy, that was for sure.

Mayhew groaned again and began to shift. He was coming round. Right, thought Coll, first thing to do was immobilise him. Then she could kill him at her leisure. She had nothing in her room to do the job, but there were ropes and chains down in the garage. The vampire had slumped in front of the door, so Coll had to grab hold of his legs to pull him out the way. It was surprisingly easy. Mayhew was strongly built and tall, but it felt like dragging a child. She tugged again. Easy! So odd . . .

Maybe vampires weighed less than people, she thought. But there was another explanation. She bent down and pulled out one of the pink plastic-covered weights she kept under her bed. She'd once planned on using them for exercise, but it had never quite happened. She held it out, palm upwards, and lifted from the elbow.

It weighed less. Definitely.

Coll ran to her door and peeped out. Silence. It was five in the morning and both her mother and brother slept like the damned. She turned, bent down, took the man in her arms and lifted him up.

'This is ridiculous,' she muttered. There was no doubt about it – her strength must have at least doubled. Maybe there was more to this immunity business than Mayhew had told her. She poked her head around the door to double-check, then ran lightly downstairs and round to the garage, carrying

Mayhew in her arms as if he had been a child of three. It was cold outside, but she hardly felt it in her excitement. She plumped him down in an old office chair against one wall, and ran to the corner where a heap of chains lay. Her dad, on one of his occasional visits to see her, had used them to lift the engine out of his motorbike some time ago.

There was a noise behind her. Mayhew was half-conscious already, trying to push himself out of his chair. Coll shoved him back and before he had time to move began wrapping the chains round and round his body, looping the links around the back of the chair. She went round his chest, over his legs, his neck and shoulders – she wanted every bit of him immobilised. At the end of it, she popped on a huge padlock from the workbench.

She paused to look at her handiwork. She was just in time. Even as she watched, Mayhew's eyes began to focus.

She had him secured – so what now? She turned to look around her for something to kill him with. Alghol had been as hard as nails, but that didn't mean the vampire was, too. Behind her, the creature groaned. He looked down at his bonds. 'You can't hold me,' he hissed. He closed his eyes, tensed himself, and pushed. He began to swell. His whole body grew, like a balloon. The chains dug in. There was a creak and a snapping noise as the links of the chain moved and dug into the wood of the chair. The monster was actually stretching the links.

He gasped for breath and relaxed. He shrugged at the chains and nodded. Already they were looser. He clenched his fists and began again.

Coll was stronger than she had been, but this was something else. She was no match for Mayhew. He had to die – fast. She ran to the workbench. There was a hammer. Good – but what to use as a stake? A chisel? It hadn't worked on Alghol, but hopefully this thing wasn't so tough. She dug about in the toolbox. There were several there. She picked out the sharpest and turned to face the vampire. He said nothing. He was too busy staring at the chisel and hammer.

'Yeah,' said Coll. She shook her weapons. 'Bummer.'

The vampire began heaving and tugging at his bonds. There was no doubt about it, she thought he looked really rather gorgeous, struggling in his chains to get free – his dark hair over his forehead, his eyes flashing and furious. It was a waste. But he was going to stretch those chains apart before long: she had no time to lose. She advanced on Mayhew, who closed his eyes and began to swell again. It was disgusting, the way he puffed up. If it wasn't for the chains, he would have been perfectly round. Any thoughts she'd had about how attractive he was had utterly vanished.

'First things first.' Coll reached into his coat pocket and removed the manuscript page he had tucked away there. 'Don't want to get my bedtime reading all messed up, do we? Right.'

Mayhew heaved at the chains so hard that the whole chair slid sideways. Coll shoved him back against the wall – she needed a firm base to strike against. She stuck a handful of oily rags from the workbench into his mouth with the end of the chisel. She wasn't sure how long it was going to take her to cut through to his black heart, but she suspected he was going to make a lot of noise while she was doing it.

She put the chisel to his chest, just under the sternum, pointing up towards his heart, and struck it with the hammer with all her strength. The vampire gasped at the blow. It went in a fraction. Blood welled around the tip. She tried again – banged and banged and banged at it. The creature howled into his rags, and heaved and pushed.

Coll checked on her handiwork. She had gashed the muscle, but she still had a long way to go.

'It's gonna be a long job, big boy,' she said. She raised the hammer and got back to work.

✻

Twenty minutes later, the vampire was still alive. Using a variety of chisels and knives, Coll had managed to hack and gouge her way through the layer of muscle over his solar plexus, and then up under the ribs all the way through to his black heart. But guess what? It was as cold and as hard as iron. The chisels just skidded off it, the knives hardly scratched the surface. She could reach right in, seize hold of it with her fist and tug at its moorings inside him as it pulsed and throbbed. But even with her foot on his chest, leaning back with all her weight, she couldn't budge it an inch.

She paused for breath. Her arms ached. Mayhew stared at her for a second, then closed his eyes and swelled up again. The chains groaned, the blood welled out of the great hole in his chest. He stretched, the chains creaked. The creature was tireless.

If only she had power! She could have done it with an electric drill, but although there was light in the garage the line to the sockets had been severed by her mother years ago, digging the garden. The nearest thing she could find was a hand drill, an old woodworking tool that was turned by hand. It was worth a go. If she got that on his heart and pushed with all her strength, it might just work – if she had time.

Coll got the drill out and fitted it up with a drill bit, the sharpest she could find. She tightened it up by hand, one eye on the vampire.

'I'm gonna drill right through your dirty heart, you bastard,' she hissed at it. Mayhew growled at her, deep in his throat, closed his eyes again and pressed against the chains. His body swelled; one of the links popped. He hung his head and gasped for breath, but only for a moment. Then he was back at it.

Coll had got the drill up into the hole in his chest and was resting the point on his beating heart when Mayhew made a noise – a kind of whimper. She looked up; he was holding his head crookedly to one side. On the wall beside him there was a small patch of light. She glanced over her shoulder. The garage had a window in the east wall with a curtain over it. Outside, the sun was rising. A ray of first light had found its way through and was striking the wall.

Surely not! She'd seen his boss in the sunlight, of course, but as the vampire had said – 'There's only one Alghol.'

She dragged the chair sideways so that Mayhew's neck was in the sunlight. At once, he tensed and screamed into his rags, and the sunlit flesh began to smoke.

'Creature of the night,' said Coll. 'Now I've got you, you lanky shit.' She ran to the window and grabbed the curtains. She turned round to look at him. There was no mistaking the look of pure terror on his face.

'Here Comes the Sun,' she said. She threw the curtains wide open.

Chapter Twelve

Those weak rays of December sunshine acted like a flame thrower on the body of the vampire. Mayhew burst into fire like dry tinder, and bubbled and hissed and smoked until all that was left was a charred mummy. It stank, too, like a mortuary fire. Coll wrapped the body in a tarp, hid it in the boot of her car, and set fire to the garage – it was the only way she could think of to explain the mess. Then she rang the fire brigade and ran back to bed, to pretend she was still sick.

Later, when the fuss had died down, and her mum had stopped wailing, she rang Beth and Louis with the good news.

It was their first real victory – a genuine defeat for the enemy. Beth and Louis were jubilant. It could be done – and their friend was still with them.

'That was a trial run,' said Louis. 'Next – Alghol himself.'

Coll drove up to join them in Whitby with the body still wrapped up in the back of her car. That night they celebrated – got in some beers, played music from their iPods on a little dock Coll kept in her car, danced, made a racket. After midnight, drunk as fools, they all passed out, Coll and Louis draped over each other, and slept the sleep of the safe, happy drunk.

In the morning, Beth got up early and walked into town to buy stuff for a fry-up, and to give the young lovers a chance to be on their own. She was charmed and delighted by the way Louis had fallen for Coll – it was as if the crises had shown her to him for the first time – and she was acutely aware of how little time they were having together. She lingered, walked by the sea; but not for very long. They were like soldiers. The fight never really stopped. When she got back, they were up and about. The caravan had been tidied up, painkillers had been taken. They ate their cooked breakfast and got on with the next thing; how to dispose of the body.

Their first idea was to dump the vampire's corpse in a flooded quarry a few miles from Todmorden, where

Louis and Beth used to go for picnics with their dad when they were small. But what if Mayhew could regenerate too? In a sudden panic they dashed out to check on the body in the boot. Sure enough, under the charred-flesh surface, fresh blood vessels were already creeping out across the hands, face and abdomen, like threads of fungi under a piece of bark on a dead tree. The vampire was already making the long journey back from death.

They all piled in the car and drove off until they found a place to park up well away from any people, where they could expose him to sunlight again. The vampire hissed, stank and shrivelled, and the tiny threads withered away. But they knew that no sooner would he arrive back in the place of the dead, than he would begin to creep back towards life. Mayhew had to be buried with a brick in his mouth. The trouble was, they only had one of those, and that was for Alghol himself. Now they had the manuscript page that the vampire had found hidden in the spine of Dee's book, they had hopes they could learn how to make more, but the whole text was in Latin — almost as hard to get through as the original book. They considered hanging on to the body and exposing it to sunlight over and over again, but that was just too dangerous. Someone might discover it and then they would have the police to worry about on top of everything else.

It was no good. They'd just have to inter Mayhew with Alghol's brick and hope that they could learn the secret of making a new one soon enough. That meant they might need access to the body again, which made dumping him in the water impractical. Burial it had to be. The site of the quarry was still good, though – it was remote, difficult to reach, and not many people knew about it. They drove back, buried him at night with the brick in his mouth, and got back to Whitby late that evening to plan their next move.

They had deprived Alghol of a soldier and, most importantly, had uncovered the secret of Dee's book. Coll was reading her way through the manuscript page that had been hidden in the spine as fast as she could, but it wasn't till two days later that she found out how to make the bricks.

It was great news. Mayhew could stay where he was and they would make a new brick for Alghol. But then Coll read on. The bricks had to be inscribed, as Pepper had said, with the phrase that they'd found on the first one. But, more importantly, they had to be made and baked at a low temperature – not fired –

with something from the vampire's own body: a strand of hair, some blood, for instance . . .

'It must be to preserve the DNA,' said Coll. Then she groaned and clutched her head.

Mayhew had been buried with the wrong brick.

Panic again. They drove all the way back to the quarry. Opening the grave by torchlight was scary and messy, and they had no idea what they would uncover. As they scraped the earth away from the head, the eyes flickered under the lids. The charred layers had already begun to slough off, and underneath them fresh pink skin was beginning to form. But the vampire was still too weak to fight back. When the torch beam fell on him he twisted his head and tried to creep away. He cried out, a low, stuttering moan. There was moisture leaking out around the eyes.

'He's weeping,' said Coll.

'He can weep for a thousand years for all I care,' said Louis savagely.

Beth looked at her brother. It was unlike him to be so vicious.

'Don't feel sorry for him,' he said. 'We can't afford to feel sorry for any of them.'

Really? thought Beth. Was it as simple as that?

Good versus evil and no questions asked. Surely nothing in life or death was ever so easy.

To make the new brick, Coll cut some scorched flesh off Mayhew's arm with a pair of sharp dissection scissors. They climbed out of the grave, shook petrol over the body, and tossed a match in after it. The fire flared up; the vampire screeched like a bird as he died again. Watching the flames, Beth wondered how many times he would have to die. Was there really no release for these souls, caught for ever between life and death, possessing neither, unable to move on? Was that Ivan's fate, too? So far they had not found so much as a hint that the disease could be reversed. She vowed then, as Mayhew wept and burned, to spend her life, if it was spared, finding a way to send the lost souls on to Glory, where they belonged.

Making the new brick wasn't hard. They bought clay, and the owners of the shop put them on to a place where they could hire the use of a kiln. Then, they had to do the whole thing over again – disinterment, digging down to the body. The stench of petrol and burned flesh floated up at them out of the earth as they got close. Mayhew tried to turn his blackened face away when they presented him with the brick.

They had to prise open his jaws and force it in. Then the body froze still. They never saw it move again.

'We'll be doing this to Alghol himself in a few weeks,' said Beth – trying the idea out to see how it felt. The answer was – unlikely. But they had taken a big step forward. John Dee had killed him in another age. Now it was their turn.

Chapter Thirteen

Christmas was coming. Beth was amazed. No one in history had ever had a time less like Christmas, but by the time they'd finished burying and reburying Mayhew, there it was, only a week away. Their parents were expecting them home but there was no way they could go. They'd probably never be forgiven, but it didn't look like there was any other choice.

'We can't hide for ever, though, can we?' said Louis. It was time to bring it on – to force the final battle. The demon continued to gain in strength, and no doubt to swell the ranks of his followers. It was never going to get any easier than it was now.

'One way or the other. Get it done,' he said.

The trouble was, they had no idea where Alghol was.

'We have bait,' pointed out Coll. 'The book and

the brick – and Beth. He'll do anything to get at her.'

Louis shook his head.

'We're all expendable now, Louis,' Beth said, and he didn't argue with her. Alghol was a massacre in this world and the next. He had to be stopped.

So – they had the bait; now all they needed was a plan. They discussed various options but each time they kept coming across the same problem. Getting to meet Alghol was going to be the easy bit. But what did they do next?

'Zap the fucker with everything we've got,' said Louis.

'We don't have any zappers,' said Coll. 'I spent over an hour trying to stake Mayhew and I couldn't do it.'

'A really big hammer. A lump hammer,' said Louis.

'I tried it. Didn't work,' said Coll.

Louis looked at her, startled. It was beginning to sink in. 'You spent an hour at it?' he asked.

Coll nodded. 'And I'm stronger than you these days, don't forget.'

'Something electric,' said Louis. 'I bet we can drill through him. What do you think?'

'What's he going to do, get himself set up nicely in a vice while we plug it in? Come on, Louis.'

Beth shook her head. 'But Dr Dee did it. How did he manage?'

Coll grinned. 'Guess what?' she said. 'He used a gun.'

The following day Coll dropped Beth and Louis off in Halifax while she drove off to visit a friend of her mother's who lived in Walsden, a little Pennine town in the hills above Todmorden. This friend was a gun owner, and Coll knew where he kept his guns. With a bit of luck he'd be out, but even if he was in – even if she had to tie him up – she was determined to bring one back.

'You'll be a wanted woman,' Beth told her.

That was the least of their worries. This was war.

The choice of Halifax wasn't random. There was no way Alghol could know they'd be there, but as it happened a mutual friend of Beth and Coll, a girl called Grace who they'd known at school in Tod, was having her birthday do there that same night. She'd moved to Halifax with her parents years ago but they'd always kept in touch with her. She was back home from uni, celebrating her birthday with a tour of the pubs and clubs in Halifax town centre.

None of them felt like a party, but at least it would be a chance to meet up with a few old friends, in safety. They could even have a few drinks. It might be their last night out. As Coll put it, you had to take your chances when you could at times like these.

She dropped them at the railway station and drove off. Beth and Louis had a few hours to kill before the party. They checked in to a hotel and popped out to get a bite to eat, then sat a while in their little room and watched TV. There was no news from Coll so far, but it was still early. Later, they wandered into town to have a look around. Christmas was there, waiting for them like a stranger at a wedding – the decorations up, trying to look jolly in the rain, people bustling on the streets and crowding in and out of the shops. They had a drink and a cup of coffee. And then – good news from Coll. Mission successful! She was on her way back in the car right now. They went back to the room and Coll turned up half an hour later in a jubilant mood, running up the stairs and banging the weapon down on the cheap hotel-room desk. It was a handgun, and only took six rounds, but it did mean that for the first time, they'd be going in properly armed.

Coll had struck lucky – the gun owner had been out and she'd had no trouble breaking in. The guns had been locked away in a cabinet, and despite her new strength she hadn't been able to get into it. But there was a handgun, loaded and ready to fire, that the owner kept under his bed in case of burglars. The friend had unwisely told her mother, and her mother had unwisely told Coll. She made off with the weapon and a nearly full box of ammunition without anyone even seeing her.

'Tomorrow, guys, we're gonna finish that bastard off,' she said, with such conviction it was almost possible to believe it. Even Alghol wouldn't be able to fight back against a modern firearm. All they had to do was get in one clear shot – even if they had to go to jail – even if they got done for murder. This time they really felt that success was in their grasp.

They went out to a bar and had a few drinks to celebrate; then it was time to go and meet Grace. There was a little debate – maybe they shouldn't go, maybe they should get an early night so as to be fresh for tomorrow. But they'd promised Grace – and why not? There was no way the demon could find them here. They went back to change into their party gear and headed out.

For some reason, Grace had decided to have an office-style party this year. They met up outside the market where she issued everyone with reindeer horns. Beth thought the whole thing was ridiculous, but Coll embraced the concept gladly.

'Great, reindeer horns,' she said. She stuck them on her head and stood there in the freezing wind,

HUNGER

beaming. Her dress was a tiny mini with little cross-straps at the back that left most of her bare. Beth, who had worn the longest, most sensible coat she had with her, wondered how she could bear to go outside like that.

'I won't be outside much and I'm expecting to be fairly heavily anaesthetised most of the time, anyway,' Coll explained.

It figured.

They trotted off round Halifax. The girls huddled in their coats, or wrapped their arms around their little dresses to keep warm, while the boys walked ahead, laughing and joking about the cold. Grace got wildly excited and made everyone swallow chasers right off – doubles in her case, since it was her birthday. As a result she was repulsively sick in Cro Bar and had to spend most of the rest of the evening being led around, supported on her friends' arms.

'It's going to be a party to remember,' said Beth.

'But not by Grace,' said Coll.

Two hours later Grace was still on her feet but out of her mind, and was busy snogging an opportunistic local lad who had turned up from somewhere. Soon he was going to offer to take her to his room; she was going to accept and throw up on his duvet.

Beth was feeling exhausted already. Her head felt

241

thick with fear about what was going to happen tomorrow – and full of other people's thoughts. Recently, since she had tried to travel down the pathway inside her, the dead had felt close to the surface. It tired her, keeping them at bay. She couldn't leave on her own – she'd promised Louis and Coll not to leave on her own. Also, her bag was too heavy. They'd made her take the gun just in case, and it was making her anxious and adding to her bad mood. She was thinking of finding a seat and sitting it out till they were ready to go when someone asked her to dance.

Beth shook her head. 'Oh, go on,' said one of the other girls, nudging her with her elbow. 'If you don't, I will.'

The boy raised his eyebrows teasingly. He was a looker. Beth couldn't help smiling back. The girl poked her again in the hip. Beth went to dance.

The next five or ten minutes were spent very pleasantly. It was good being at the centre of some-one's attention again. They danced, chatted a little, told each other about themselves. His name was Joz and he lived locally. He was at uni studying art, just back for Christmas. He tried to buy her a drink but the bar was crowded, and she didn't want to wait that long for it. He tried it on a bit during a smoochie, but not in too pushy a way – just enough so she knew he was really pretty interested. She agreed he could ring her, and he tapped her number into his phone.

Coll grabbed her when he went to the loo.

'Who's the cutie?' she asked.

'Name's Joz,' said Beth. 'What do you think?'

Coll nodded. 'He's pretty,' she said. Beth smiled, pleased with herself. 'Just – you know. Stay in the crowd, OK?' added Coll.

'What do you think, I'm going to go off and give him one round the back of the building? Do I look like you?'

'You have the gun?'

Beth nodded. She didn't want to think about that, though. It was their night off. 'I'd know if there was anything going on. Mum would let me know somehow.' She looked around. 'Where's Louis? Hey – that's Mel he's dancing with, isn't it?'

Coll scowled. 'Yeah. Miss Minging 2012. I know he doesn't fancy her. Not even when she does *that*,' she said, glaring at the couple.

Joz appeared across the room and headed towards them.

'He's coming back for more,' said Coll.

'Don't sound so surprised.'

'Seeing him again?'

'He took my number,' said Beth. She beamed. He'd taken her number. A boy was interested in her.

'Yum.'

'Yeah, innit?'

'See? I told you. Boys like a handful.'

'Thanks.'

'Sorry, was I being tactless? I never quite know.'

Joz pushed his way over to them.

'This is my friend Coll,' said Beth.

Coll eyed the boy up approvingly. A bit on the short side – but perfectly formed.

'Time for one more?' asked Joz.

Yeah, time for one more. It was a smooch. Beth was rediscovering that she liked smooching. Then she could go home.

They danced; Beth let Joz lean into her and wondered if he was going to try to kiss her. If he did, she was going to let him. She leaned her head on his shoulder and caught a whiff, a stink of rotting meat. She lifted her head up for a second – where was that coming from? At the same moment, Joz tightened his hold on the back of her neck. He pushed a finger against one of the vertebrae so hard that her legs trembled under her. She would have fallen if he hadn't been holding her up. Distantly, far, far away, she could hear her mother screaming; too late. The screaming rose suddenly to a deafening pitch; then it closed down abruptly.

'Noisy Mama,' the demon said. He pulled back her head as if she was a puppet and smiled into her face, waltzing her round as if she was still dancing. This was how far he had moved in just one week since they had seen him in the library. He was young and beautiful, and he could gag her mother at will.

He pressed a little more tightly on the vertebra in her neck. 'I could pop it out with one finger if I wanted to,' he told her. 'I could push it right into your throat and make you swallow it. But you wouldn't be able to, Beth, because you'd be a quadriplegic. Now, if you don't want some tart from the NHS changing your nappies for the rest of your life, keep quiet and come with me.'

He walked her out of the bar and on to the street. It was late, but there were still people about. Beth wondered if she should scream, but she didn't dare. Every few steps he dug his finger into her spine and bent her spinal nerve – she could feel the pressure right down her back. The gun waited in her bag. She tried to move her arm experimentally, to be ready when the chance came, but he must have been crushing some nerve or other because she was unable to lift it at all.

It hurt so much that she could hardly breathe. He could do exactly what he wanted with her.

Alghol led her round to a small backstreet behind the bar, where he positioned her under a street light. He had changed out of all recognition. Where he had been old, now he was young; where he had been disgusting, now he was beautiful. Now that they were on their own he seemed to release himself from within and shone with vigour and youth, with grace, strength and self-belief. He was the most beautiful person Beth had ever seen.

'Look at me,' he crooned. 'How can you resist me now?' He spun her round, so that her back was up against the wall and leaned into her like a lover. 'You cannot,' he said. He stared at her with ancient eyes. Suddenly, he pressed forward and kissed her, full on the mouth. His tongue slipped between her lips. He tasted sweet – just for a moment. Then Beth tasted what he really was, and she gagged.

'You don't find me attractive?' he said, as if he was surprised. 'Are you frigid, do you think?'

'How did you find us?' she asked.

'Coll told me, of course.' He waited, watching her reaction. 'Hehehe. I'm lying,' he confessed. 'Your friend sent Ivan an invite by email. I think maybe they had a little, ah, liaison at some point.'

None of them had known that Ivan and Grace had ever met each other, let alone slept together, but it was typical of him to have made it with one of their friends without any of them even knowing. They'd been careless. 'What do you want?' she begged.

'I want the book. I want the brick. But, most of all Beth, I want you. I'd quite like my servant back, too. I rather liked Don. Where is he?'

'Where you'll never find him.'

'Oh, Beth, but I will, sweetheart, you know I will. You can't defeat me. What are you? Just a bunch of kids.'

As he spoke he reached out and took the bag in his hand. He took it from her, to her shame, without her even resisting, and opened it up.

'I thought it was little heavy. A shooter. How disappointing. You were really seriously trying to kill me, weren't you?' he said.

Alghol leered up at her, opened his mouth wider and wider, like a toad, until his head seemed about to fall into two, and dropped the gun into his maw. He swallowed it whole. Then he dropped his hand to Beth's backside, took hold of one cheek and squeezed so hard that she thought he might burst open the skin and stick his fingers into the raw flesh.

She would have screamed, but his other hand was clamped tight over her mouth.

He leaned fiercely close to her ear and hissed into it. 'You will learn to respect me.' Then he controlled himself and smiled. 'I like this age. I will take this age. This will be my age.' He pulled back and studied her face. 'We will be lovers. I offer you – eternal life! Wealth, power, everything you could dream of. Why would anyone say no to that?'

'Because it involves murder,' Beth gasped.

'Your lives are such little things. I have had very many of your little lives.'

He smiled again, then opened his mouth and from him, from inside, a myriad of voices began to murmur, then shout. It was a babble of voices from across all the ages.

'We are Legion,' hissed the demon, 'And our age is upon us. Beth! Why be in a hurry to die? Let the others go there first.'

Along the road came some footsteps. A couple, arm in arm, walking past, a boy and a girl, on their way home perhaps, taking a short cut.

'Shall we kill them?' asked Alghol. 'It won't take long. You get used to it so quickly.'

Beth shook her head. 'Then kiss me,' he told her. He pressed her into the wall and mouthed her face. She turned her head away. 'Put your arms around me and kiss me or I will kill them, right now,' he hissed. Beth did as she was told. He tasted of rot; she had to concentrate hard not to gag on his lips and tongue.

The couple drew level. Beth had closed her eyes instinctively as she and Alghol kissed, but opened them as the other two drew level. The boy was watching her: it was Louis.

Louis raised his eyebrows questioningly. Beth rolled her eyes and nodded slightly. Louis stepped back. Coll took something from under her coat – a fire extinguisher. She nodded at Beth, who ducked suddenly as Coll drove the metal cylinder straight at the back of the demon's head. He was quick – maybe he had heard something. He moved sideways, but not far enough, and the blow caught him on the side of his head, smashing his face into the wall. He sank down; Louis rushed him with a kitchen knife, and managed to deliver a blow with all his force to the monster's stomach. The knife glanced harmlessly off him and scraped against the wall. Alghol twisted round and shoved Louis backwards, so hard that he went skidding across the road and banged into the wall on the other side.

Beth flung herself sideways out of reach. Coll went in at Alghol again, but the demon sidestepped her, grabbed her by the hair, and banged her head against the wall. She flopped down at once. He spun her round, seized hold of her dress at the back, then turned and ran straight up the sheer wall in front of them, using his feet and only one hand; Coll hung limply from the other. He was like a monkey, or a squirrel, dashing from side to side, finding footholds not just on the sills, but on the cracks in between the bricks on his way up.

He reached the top and peered down as Beth and Louis were picking themselves up from the ground. Coll still hung limply in his hand. He dangled her over the street and shook her gently. 'Shall I drop her?' he called. 'No? Then I'll make a deal. The book, the brick and my servant back. Then your friend lives. If not, I'll drink her blood, and then I'll drink yours too. Agreed? I think so. And Beth. You, too. You are the gateway and one world is no longer big enough for me.'

Without waiting for an answer, he disappeared up onto the roof. Above them, there was a dark shadow as the demon jumped across the street at roof level. Then he was gone.

666

Coll came to in the back seat of a large car, her head thumping. Alghol was sitting next to her, smoking a cigarette, while a young woman in front drove. Coll kept still, peering out of the window to try and work out where they were going. They were back in Manchester, she realised suddenly. She knew this part of town, more or less; maybe that would come in useful when she tried to escape. Soon they pulled up outside a large semi. The driver sat quietly, waiting for orders.

Alghol had moved up in the world, Coll reflected, from the days when he had been holed up in a derelict old shop living off corpse flesh. Now he was young, beautiful and powerful. His new residence wasn't a mansion but, considering he'd only been out of the ground just under three weeks, it wasn't bad – a big semi in an expensive part of the posh suburb of West Didsbury, just a short walk from the shops.

'Will you walk nicely, or do we have to do it the hard way?' he asked Coll; then he shook his head. 'I can't be arsed,' he said. He reached over, took her skull in his hand and squeezed. There was a blinding flash of pain; then she passed out.

Coll came to again in a kitchen diner, knocked through to form one long room. She was sitting on the floor. Her hands were free, but there was an iron collar around her neck, bolted to a pillar behind her. She tugged at it experimentally. It was immovable.

'You aren't going anywhere,' a voice said. Coll looked up. It was the young woman who had been driving the car. She smiled, showing vampire's teeth.

'That brick is going to taste vile,' said Coll. 'I'll see to it myself. I may even smear dog shit on it for you.'

'No, you won't. You know you won't,' the woman said. 'You're going to die.' The certainty in her voice made Coll quail but she didn't show it, just shook her head.

'Loser,' she sneered. Then the door opened and the demon himself came into the room.

It was the first time she'd got a good look at him in the light. He was so beautiful it took her breath away. He shone with it. Sitting on the floor and gazing up at him, Coll felt her jaw hang open. When he stared down at her she looked away, as if to even look at something so lovely was vulgar in some way.

'Aren't I?' he said. 'Aren't I just?' He nodded to the woman. 'You can go now,' he said.

The woman paused, and glanced sideways at Coll. She was jealous. She didn't want to leave Alghol on his own with a pretty girl. 'You look more beautiful than ever tonight,' she told him.

Alghol smiled. 'We shall have eternity together. I promise.'

'He's lying, you know he's lying,' said Coll. The

woman snarled at her — literally: she sounded like a dog. But she did as she was told, leaning across to peck Alghol on the cheek before she left.

Alghol smiled. 'Women,' he said, and rolled his eyes. He crossed the room to the back of the kitchen and put his hand on the handle of a door, leading through to a conservatory behind the house. There was a noise from inside. 'Allow me to introduce,' he said. He opened the door and stepped back. 'You two know one another already, I think. But look. He's all grown-up now.'

Something heavy shuffled up to the door. A hand appeared and grasped the side of the frame. Coll stared at it in fascination. The palm was thick and solid, almost human, but the fingers had shrunk and turned into brutal-looking stubs. The nails had curled up, thickened, and turned yellow. It had been a human hand once. Now it was more or less an articulated paw.

A figure slouched in through the door on all fours. Ivan was more than half hyena now, from the high spotted shoulders, to the grinning mouth, the huge pointed head and oddly bulging eyes. The teeth, which showed through the black-lipped mouth, were stubby and thick, like stunted tusks. If Coll hadn't seen him halfway through this transition, she wouldn't have recognised him at all.

'Ivan,' she said, trying to keep her voice even. 'How you doing?'

Ivan turned his head to look at her. The brow furrowed slightly. He stared at her for a while, then lunged suddenly forward towards her. Despite herself, Coll screamed but Ivan was pulled up short by a chain around his neck. Like Coll, he was on a lead.

'Don't do that,' said the demon. 'He tends to think things on the floor are food, especially when they scream. He's usually right. Let's hang on to life a little longer, shall we? These last few hours aren't going to be fun, but it's better than being dead. Believe me, I know. Dead is a good deal less than any sort of fun at all.' For a second, he looked sad. 'And of course, if you hang on . . . who knows, you may even escape!' He stared at her, making his eyes big and round, then laughed. 'Just kidding,' he said. 'You really are going to die. If you try to escape, I'll kill you now instead of later. That's about the best I can offer.'

Staring fixedly at Coll, Ivan let himself down on his belly.

'Hungry,' said Alghol. 'He's always hungry. That's all he ever is.' He shook his head and suddenly aimed a vicious kick at Ivan's head. It caught him on the small bones at the corner of his skull. Ivan screamed — a dreadful noise as it was still in his own voice, about the only thing of himself that he had left. He cringed onto the floor, holding his head in his hands and moaning.

'Sorry, I sorry, sorry sorry sorry . . .' he moaned.

Alghol sneered. 'Sorry sorry sorry. Its name might as well be "Sorry",' he said. He shook his head. 'Four hundred years in a box and when I get out I get this for company. You idiot cur.'

Ivan cowered back as Alghol bent to the floor. But the demon was only after Coll's bag, which he picked up and rummaged through. Coll looked at the wreck of what had once been her friend. Cautiously, she reached out a hand.

'I wouldn't do that if I were you,' said Alghol.

Coll ignored him. 'Hey, Ivan,' she said softly. 'Remember me? It's Coll. We had some good times, hey? Remember when I stayed over at yours . . . the first time? Hey? I was still in sixth form, you liked that. Hey, Ivan, come on, it's OK . . .'

Ivan peered at her sideways – then darted out a hand, grabbed hold of her and started to haul her towards him. Coll let out a shriek and tried to pull back, but he had ten times her strength.

'Told you,' said Alghol. He turned away. He took Coll's phone from her bag and started scrolling through it.

Coll rapidly reached the end of her chain and the

iron collar tightened around her neck. Her face swelled up and turned red. Ivan wrenched forward and reached for her face with his teeth, but she was still out of reach. Coll gurgled. 'Hey, Ivan, you're hurting me.' Very carefully, she put her other hand out and tried to ease a finger under his. Ivan paused and watched her curiously. 'We're friends,' she groaned, squeezing the words out from under the metal around her neck. 'Mates. It's me. It's Coll. Remember me, Ivan?'

He looked at her and shook his head.

'Sure you do!'

Confused, Ivan released the pressure of his hand. Coll darted back, Ivan jumped at her again – too late. She was out of reach. She massaged her neck. It felt as if he'd been about to pull her head clean off.

'Fool,' said Alghol in disgust. He found a number on the phone and pressed dial.

There was a moment's silence while he waited for an answer. 'I'll send you details of how to get near here on email,' said Alghol into the phone. It was evidently on voicemail. 'Bring your phone, and I'll guide you the rest of the way. Tomorrow, about one, shall we say? The book and the brick. You can let me know where my servant is when you get here.'

He turned the phone off and looked down at Coll.

'Fancy some sex?' he said. 'I believe you like that sort of thing. More interesting than spending the night with Ivan, I think I can guarantee that. I could grant you a few last wishes.'

'Funny thing, I'm right off my game just now.'

'But you have to fill the time,' said Alghol. 'Eternity is so long,' he said. 'We have to fill it as best we can. There's no way out. Just a billion, billion miles of hunger.' He stared at her with such an expression that she wondered if he might cry. But he shook off the mood and smiled again.

'Please yourself,' he said. 'I have other entertainment upstairs. Right. Better feed the dog before bed.'

'Alghol,' said Coll suddenly. 'Ghul, Ghula. Gul of the waste.' It was worth a try, wasn't it? Damning him with his own name. The demon turned to her with a snarl. 'Vetala. Baitai, Betail. Ghula!' she yelled, and to her delight he groaned and staggered. Yes! 'Vetala, Baitai. Ghula!' she cried, and he tumbled down to his knees. But which one was it? Already he was turning towards her, groaning, his hand reaching for her throat. 'Ghula!' she cried. He stopped. His face creased in pain. 'Ghula!' she yelled again. 'So that's your name, you piece of piss. Ghula, Ghula!' she yelled. The demon shuddered, put his hands around his throat and, as Coll called the name over and over, curled up in pain. A series of tremendous spasms ran through him. Finally he lay still, and slowly, painfully, his eyes moved to meet hers.

'But . . . I'm . . . only . . . joking,' he whispered. He lay staring at her a moment then jumped to his feet. Despite herself, Coll bent her head and sobbed. 'Disappointment,' he said. 'So much harder to bear after a little lift, I always think. Hey ho. Easy come, easy go.' He smiled and chuckled at his own joke. 'The last time I did that was back in 1605, to John Dee. You should have seen his face! Then I ate his wife. Now then, where was I? Ah yes. Feed the dog.'

He went to the fridge and took out a meaty bone, which he threw on the floor. Ivan took it in his jaws, with a grunt of satisfaction, and began to splinter it between his great yellow teeth.

'A human femur,' said the demon, seeing Coll's expression. 'Cows' are too thick, birds' are too thin. A human bone is just right to crunch all up!' He stood and watched her for a moment longer, then turned to go.

'Mine's upstairs,' he said.

'Can I go to the toilet?' asked Coll.

'Mmmmmmm – no. Tell you what, though.' He bent down to Ivan and unclipped the chain from his collar. 'You two seem so familiar, you can have a chat.' 'Old times' sake.' He smiled. 'Is it going to be a long night, or a short one? I'll find out in the morning, I guess.' The demon smiled, turned the light off, and left the room. A moment later Coll heard someone whimper upstairs.

It was still dark outside. Down on the floor, the shadows were so deep that she could hardly see anything. She had the feeling that Ivan was staring at her, though, while he devoured his bone. After ten minutes or so the crunching stopped. There was a pause, and then he began to growl slightly.

'Hey, Ivan,' she said. 'How's it hanging? You OK?'

Coll sensed shadow creeping towards her in the darkness.

'Where's your bone, boy?' she asked. In answer came a deep growl.

'Finished already? Bummer, eh?' The huge shovel head swung suddenly into view and she had to stifle a scream. His eyes shone a pale green, reflecting the dull lamplight from outside.

'Ivan,' she whispered. 'Hi.'

Ivan growled deep in his throat, walked up to her, lowered his head to her face and sniffed.

'Remember me, Ivan? It's Coll. Hey – what are you doing tomorrow night? Fancy a few beers?'

Ivan paused and looked closely at her.

'Beers? Remember? You like beer.'

Slowly, like a rock moving, Ivan nodded.

'Hey – we could start now. You want me to go the fridge and get some beer right now?'

'Urrrrm,' growled Ivan. It was difficult to tell, but he seemed to be smiling.

'Doesn't that bastard give you any beer, then?' Coll said.

Sadly, Ivan shook his head.

'I'll get some for you.' She made as if to get up, then laughed weakly. 'Hey, guess what? That bastard has tied me up. Can you think of any way I can get loose so I can get to that beer? We can do that if we work together, can't we? What do you reckon?'

Chapter Fourteen

Beth was in the loo back at the house in Fallowfield when she heard her phone go. She missed the call and rang back at once, but it was already on answerphone. 'Let me speak to her,' she begged, but there was no reply. She was starting up her laptop as Louis came into the room.

The email was already there, telling them to go to the Burton Road in West Didsbury. The demon would guide them from there.

'Didsbury. The last place I'd have thought a demon would live,' said Louis.

'Well, where would he live?'

'I dunno. House of Commons?'

'Nah – Whalley Range,' said Beth – an area of Manchester where Louis had once been mugged. Louis shook his head. Neither of them laughed.

'Lou, what are we going to do?' said Beth.

Louis shook his head. 'He would have to take her, wouldn't he?' They both felt lost without Coll. She was the one who always had a plan. 'Have you heard from Mum?' he asked hopefully.

'Nothing.'

'He got past her.'

'Not into my head.'

'She's still there, though?'

'I heard her call, but it was too late.'

'Can you reach her?' asked Louis, anxiously.

Beth shook her head. 'I've been trying,' she said defensively. 'It's dangerous.'

'You did last time.'

'In the caravan she came to me. The time before that – that wasn't Mum. It was . . . where the dead go. She was there, I think, but I couldn't find her. She told me to go. I could have died.' She chewed at a hangnail. They'd lost the gun without firing a single shot. Coll was gone. They'd been rubbish. 'Do we meet him?' she asked. 'If we go, he'll have all of us and that will be that. There'll be no one to stop him.'

'How can we not go? It's Coll,' demanded Louis.

'What if it's a trap?'

'Of course it's a trap!'

'Then we can't put ourselves at risk like that. She

may already be dead,' said Beth. 'He didn't let me speak to her.'

'But maybe not,' said Louis. He wanted to cry. They'd only just got her back, and now she was in danger again. He put his head in his hands and tried to think. 'In the caravan that time,' he said. 'Mum was trying to tell you something, don't you think? Maybe she's been trying all the time. But now we've run out of time. You're going to have to go back and find her.'

'I don't know how, Louis. I've tried. It doesn't work.'

Louis looked steadily at her. 'So do we just wait?' he said. 'Or do you have another plan?'

The only controlled experience of exploring down into herself that Beth had ever had was with the hypnotherapist, Charles Peters. Back then it had been Alghol who'd been waiting for her in the channels of her mind, but things had changed since then. This time, maybe she would find her mother instead.

She got Louis to wait in the room with her, in case she got into trouble. Then she sat herself down on an upright chair and tried to relax.

This scared her. It was a journey into the darkness. The dead lived there. But her mother was one of them. That was what she had to hang on to.

She let her thoughts drift back to the vision that the hypnotherapist had given her the last time she had contacted that place. The slow walk through her front door back at home in Todmorden . . . into the hall . . . the revelation of the door in the floor that led to a place more real than she had ever imagined possible.

Beth shifted on her chair and moaned slightly, but forced her mind back, back to the door in the floor . . . the doorway to death. It appeared again in her mind's eye, alarmingly clear. She could even make out the detail of the paintwork on the skirting boards along the hall.

Her arms twitched slightly, as she bent to lift open the door. Below her, the steps led down into a soft light. She went down a couple then paused. This was as far as she remembered going.

'Anyone there?' she called softly.

She paused, waiting for an answer. There was none. She carried on down the steps. Beside her, Louis rose from his chair and stood over her, a chisel and hammer firmly in his hand. He wasn't sure that he had the strength, but he would try – in the name of God, he would try – to kill his own sister if he had to.

Calmly, but suddenly, Beth opened her eyes. It made him jump.

'Well?' Louis asked. Then; 'Is it you, Beth?'

'It's me,' she said. She sat up and shook her head. 'There's no one there. Sorry, Lou. We're on our own.'

Louis sank back into his chair. 'We can't go, then,' he said. 'We still have the book and the brick. He'll want them. It means we can't go.'

Neither of them could bear to be parted, so they shared a bed that night, like they had when they'd been small, years ago. Before he went to sleep, Louis said his prayers, something he had been doing more of late. If he had been starting to have doubts as he got older, these events had chased them away altogether. If there was evil, there must be good. If not, what was the point? Louis believed that there was a point and that the point was God. Alghol was not just the enemy of Mankind – he was the enemy of the Divinity, too. Surely God would find a way to help them in their hour of need!

Although he had stopped kneeling to pray years ago, this time he got down by the bedside to bow his head and put his hands together while Beth peered over the duvet and smiled at him. It made him feel like a child, but perhaps that was a good way to approach God. He knew in his heart that God already knew if, and how, and why He was going to act against the demon; but prayer, perhaps, had some effect. He could only hope. It made him feel better, if nothing else. When he was done, he climbed into bed, kissed his sister, and fell quickly into a restless sleep.

He awoke an hour or two later to find Beth sitting on the side of the bed. She smiled – an odd smile, he thought. She put her hand on his face – and the movement wasn't hers.

Louis froze. 'Who are you?' he croaked. But he already knew.

'Louis.' She smiled. 'My big boy. My big, beautiful boy, all grown-up, and I missed it all. So sorry, Louis. So sorry.'

Louis's breath caught in his throat. She'd come to him. All these years she had been there for Beth. Finally, she had come to him, too. He felt so grateful for this stolen moment.

'I wish . . .' he began. But now she was here, he didn't know what to say. He reached out to take her hand.

'I wish, too, Louis. I wish, I wish.'

She stiffened and winced.

'I can't stay here. I have to be there . . . for Beth. It hurts me,' she said, and she shook her head as if to chase something away. 'Louis, listen. We're going to stop this thing. We can send him away for ever. Do you understand?'

Louis shook his head. How could he understand?

'You must,' she said urgently. She winced again, in pain. 'I stayed as close as I could . . . You have no idea.' Her eyes suddenly turned inward and she started to babble in a low voice, as if she was being swept away by a tide of other ghosts. She grimaced, and forced herself back.

'So sorry, Louis,' she said again. 'So, so sorry.'

'It wasn't your fault' he said. More had been taken from her than from him, but it was himself he felt sorry for.

'It's a disease, Louis. He's not a demon. He's a man. It is a disease of the soul. Understand.' She closed her eyes and began to pant. 'The light,' she said. 'The light is Glory. He needs to move on. We must help him on his way.'

'What light? I don't understand! The light I saw coming from Beth?'

'Yes! The dead pass on. So can he. Beth can pass his soul to me and I can take him on with me, on to the light, to Glory. But Louis, he has to want to go, and I don't know if he will. You see? We can help him, but he has to leave of his own free will. If not, you must kill him.'

'But how?' begged Louis. 'We lost the gun. I can hardly even break his skin. What chance do I have?'

'I've brought help.' Suddenly, she smiled; it was a smile like a death's head. But she seemed to be genuinely amused. 'Remember the children of the Hydra's teeth,' she said.

Louis smiled. That was more like the mother he remembered. '*Jason and the Argonauts*,' he said.

'You loved that film. Yes. It's the same with Alghol. A hundred centuries of lost souls, destroyed by him. It's from them that he takes his strength, but through Beth we can turn them against him. Look at me, Louis. This is what you have to do. Look at me. Look at her – into her eyes. The dead are with you, too.'

She reached out with her hands, seized his face and forced him to stare right at her, deep into her eyes – into the realm of death. Louis struggled, but was unable to resist. He was falling, falling down; and there they were, the hideous dead, a hundred thousand rotting corpses, never free from the grip of the flesh, never able to escape the pain of death. A hundred thousand souls trapped in their own deaths, screaming at him, yelling at him to help them . . .

'The dead will help the living if the living will help the dead,' hissed his mother. 'Understand!'

Louis gasped, struggled, and at last managed to push her away. The vision receded, and she slumped to one side.

'Mum,' he gasped. She was falling down off the bed, trying weakly to climb back next to him. He helped her up, and she sat there for a moment, staring at the wall with her dreadful eyes, panting. Finally she turned to look at him again.

'Goodbye, Louis,' she said, and she laid herself down next to him.

'Don't go!' But she lay still. 'Mum?' He shook her shoulder. He had one more question for her. She stirred, like someone half asleep. 'Mum, tell me – this is what God wants, isn't it? I'm doing this for Him, aren't I? Is it all right – you know – to kill it?'

With a visible effort, she turned to look at him. Her face looked dark and woozy. She shook her head.

'There is no God, Louis,' she whispered. 'Glory – but no God. Just get this done . . . and live your life. I love you, Louis.'

She was going. 'I love you too. I missed you, Mum,' he told her, because he knew this was his only chance to say it.

'Love you . . . love you . . . so sorry, Louis . . .'

A shudder went through her body. She was gone. Louis rolled onto his back and looked up at the ceiling, his eyes full of tears. There. She'd come to him, too, in the end. And now where was he? No mother. And no bloody God after all.

'Great,' he said, wiping his eyes. 'That's just fucking dandy, then, isn't it?'

Chapter Fifteen

They took Coll's car to the Burton Road at one, and then rang her phone. A young woman gave them instructions towards West Didsbury, and they pulled up outside the demon's house fifteen minutes later.

'I don't like it,' said Louis.

Beth looked sideways at him. 'Mother knows best,' she said.

Louis was furious. So the plan was to hand the demon over to the light – just like that? No arguments, no punishment. Just here you go – Glory on a plate. Thanks for the thousands of years of misery and darkness you've caused. Have a nice time! Once he'd thought that a thousand years in a box wasn't bad enough for Alghol, but if the alternative was Glory – go for it.

Beth sighed and looked over to the house, standing

there in the dull winter light. One more large semi in West Didsbury. Inside there was a real live demon, and it had their friend. Pretty soon, she thought, it was going to have them as well.

'Happy Christmas, house,' she said. 'Happy Christmas, Beth. What do you want for Christmas? Oh, I'll have eternity in a box. No problem. It won't hurt a bit.'

Louis patted his thigh. He had an iron spike tucked down his jeans leg. It didn't make him feel all that safe but, as he'd recently discovered, it was better than faith.

'Have you thought about what happens if he bites you?' he asked. 'You're the one with your belly button or whatever in the next world. What sort of monster will you turn into? Did Mum tell you that?'

Beth shook her head. She had no idea. 'He will try to bite me. Of course he will. He wants my gift to serve him.' She shrugged. 'I have Mum protecting me. She can hide my soul. I don't think he can get me. We'll see.'

Louis looked at her. 'Do you believe it, Beth? You really think we can send him out of this world for ever?'

'You know what I think, Louis?' she said. 'I think we don't stand a chance. That thing in there is thousands of years old. It's killed God knows how many people, it's turned Ivan into a monster. It eats souls. It made me dig it up, for God's sake, after being stuck in the ground for four hundred years. We are so stuffed. So let's just go for it, shall we? Nothing we can do is a match for that thing, so let's just go for the jackpot.'

Again Louis touched the metal of the spike, warm against his thigh. 'We can win, Beth,' he said. 'We have to win.'

'We're going in there to die,' she said.

'Let's go and die, then,' said Louis. 'And let's take that bastard with us.' He got out of the car, waited for Beth, and then locked the door behind them.

'In case someone nicks it,' he said. 'I'm not paying for a taxi to get home.'

666

The door was opened to them by a young woman. She stood in the shadows, staring coolly at them, and for a moment Beth thought they must have come to the wrong place. Then she smiled, showing her fangs, and stood to one side to let them in.

Inside, the house was poorly lit, with heavy curtains and blinds drawn against the pale December light outside. It stank, too, of blood and death. Beth thought it might be another vison, but from the way Louis choked and put his hand to his mouth she knew it was real. The woman led the way to the back of the house and opened a door. The stink increased, and was added to by the rank smell of dog. She stood aside to let them through to the kitchen.

'The General will join you shortly,' she told them, before closing the door behind them and leaving them to it.

It was very dark in there, with all the windows covered up and just a small light coming from above the cooker hob on one side. From the deep shadows came a deep, low growl. Louis flicked a switch, and a neon light in the ceiling blinked rapidly on and off, without catching. But it was enough to show them the dreadful figure of Ivan on the floor at the far end of the room, climbing to his feet and starting towards them, caught in the strobe of the flashing light.

Quickly, Louis drew out the spike from his jeans and pushed Beth behind him. Ivan surged forward, but stopped short with a jerk after less than a metre. He was chained to the floor.

Across from the cooker was a table with a lamp on it. Louis walked over, keeping a careful eye on Ivan, who strained at his chain, growling ferociously, and turned the lamp on.

They were standing in a large kitchen diner. To their right was a long dining table, with the kitchen to the left. There was a door at the back leading out to a darkened conservatory. Ivan blinked at the light, which fell directly on him, grimacing and clawing at his collar in frustration at not being able to get at them.

'Ivan,' said Beth. He turned to her voice with a snarl and then stopped suddenly, staring at her. Whether it was with recognition or not, she had no idea as his face no longer held any clues to what he was feeling. His mouth was fixed in a permanent grin that meant nothing, his eyes bulged like stones but at least he'd stopped growling.

Beth turned off the flickering neon light and looked around her. There was no sign of either her friend or her enemy. The demon was toying with them, no doubt – letting the fear build before he showed himself. If that was his game, it was working.

She looked over at Ivan again. Gradually he lowered himself to the ground and laid his head on his paws as if he was resting. But his eyes were open and he was following them both closely. Beth swallowed. Her throat was bone dry. The stink of flesh and rotting meat was overwhelming, and she felt sick with fear, but her head was clear and she knew exactly what she had to do.

'Louis,' she said. 'You need to kill him now.'

'What?' Louis was horrified. Kill Ivan? That hadn't been part of the plan.

'It's our chance. If Alghol won't let me send him on, we'll still have to fight him. At least this way he won't have Ivan to help him.'

Louis stared at her. What had happened to his sweet little sister? But she was right. He reached down and pulled out the spike from his jeans.

'I might not be able to. You know how tough the others were.'

'Try.'

Louis edged forward. Ivan growled, stood up, tensed, and strained at his chain to meet him. As Louis got closer, the growling increased. By the time he ended up just a short way out of Ivan's reach he could feel the noise shaking his stomach.

How to do it? Through the eye, perhaps. Carefully, Louis lifted the spike and took aim. He steadied his hand. Ivan stared up at him, his lips curling, apparently unaware of what he was about to do.

'A little murder in the dark. I approve. But perhaps the victim is not quite the right choice.'

A door had opened at the back of the kitchen, and Alghol himself stepped in. He had been waiting in the conservatory in the dark, watching and listening to them. He took three rapid steps towards Louis, quickly relieved him of the iron spike and shoved him backwards towards Beth.

The demon was shorter than Beth remembered.

He had an odd, slightly lop-sided face, but somehow it only added to his beauty. He was so full of grace and certainty – the charisma of power – that it took her breath away. But then she caught a whiff of him, of his ancient evil, of his greed, of the stink he made in two worlds, and she gagged and took a step back.

Alghol scowled. 'You won't be like that when you're one of mine,' he said. He sneered at their shocked faces. 'Are you here to rescue your friend? I don't think you are. You're here for the same reason as all the others. To feed me.'

As he spoke, Ivan had begun to lick the demon's feet. Casually, Alghol kicked out at him, catching him in the ribs. Ivan whimpered and scurried back out of the way. Beth was filled with fury at the casual way he hurt someone he had made to love him. She tried to hide her feeling and walked up to him as if she was about to talk. Then, at the last moment, she pulled a knife and slashed at his face.

Louis ran to help her, but Alghol sidestepped her easily, caught her by the arm, and in a second had her own knife at her throat. Louis stopped in his tracks.

'Ah, Beth.' Alghol smiled and touched his finger to the side of her face. 'So keen to kill.' He twisted her round and turned her to face him. 'How like me you are already. I told you – it doesn't take long to get used to it. We shall be lovers soon. We shall control eternity.'

'Not like you,' insisted Louis. 'Nothing like you. She's trying to stop the killing. It's just more fresh meat to you.' As he spoke he took off his rucksack and undid it. His spike was gone, but he had other weapons to use.

'You flatter yourselves with your good intentions. Your kind has persecuted my kind for aeons, but this is our age. Now I have Beth with me, I shall rule the worlds and death shall have no dominion.' He laughed. 'But what will the poets do, when everyone is dead?' he asked.

Beth struggled to speak. It was time to talk, to make her offer – but in her terror she was unable to speak. Now that he was no longer bothering to hide from her, she could see past his beauty to the horror and disease beneath. Despite his apparent youth, despite his power and glory, his soul was vile, stinking of corpse flesh and greed. He was so full of it that it made her catch her breath.

Alghol groaned as if he could see himself with her eyes. 'Only you can see me – only you. Yes, yes. The terrible hunger of the dead for life. But Beth – once in a while, some of us make it back. There is no cost, not even this, that any of us wouldn't gladly pay to be here for just a few more hours of life. For the dead, you people are the food of the gods.'

Beth fought against her gagging throat. 'You aren't even dead,' she spat. In answer, he seized her hair, bent her head back and smacked her neck so that her legs failed beneath her and he had to hold her up. Again, Louis ran forward, but Alghol swatted him lightly away. He laughed. 'You want me to resist my desire for her? I never resisted any desire in my life. With Beth by my side, I shall feed on the souls of the dead as well as on those of the living. We shall be like gods. We will feed until at last there is no more hunger, and we shall never die.'

Beth tried to twist her head around to meet his eyes, but his arm was as immovable as rock. 'There is no death for you,' she said. 'And no end to your hunger, until you cross over.'

The demon looked startled. For a moment he seemed to be almost afraid of her; then he shook it off. 'First things first,' he said. He pushed her away from him and held out his hand. 'The brick.'

Louis stood up and lifted his rucksack. He glanced at Beth.

'Oh, I see,' said Alghol. 'This is the moment when you make your move. Another chisel, is it, Louis? Something like that. Let's make it easy for you.' He opened his arms and waited. 'Well? What are you waiting for? I am at your mercy.'

'Where's Coll? We agreed to swap for Coll,' Louis said.

'Coll. Yes. Let me see. Oh, I know. She's in the fridge.'

The demon walked to the fridge and opened it. He reached in and suddenly swung round to face them. In his hand, held up by the hair, was Coll's head. It caught them so utterly by surprise – the shock of it, the dead eyes, the expression of horror and the pain she had died in – that they both yelled and fell back.

'I'm afraid her conversational skills weren't as good as she thought they were. Catch!' He flung the head at Louis, who yelled again and shied away. It hit the floor with a sickening thud and a dull crack, and rolled across the tiles, to rest against the skirting, staring blindly at them. One of Coll's eyes was missing and a part of her cheek had been torn off. As the head landed, Ivan jumped to fetch it, like a dog after a ball. It lay just beyond his teeth but he reached out and pulled it to him with his paw, and closed his mouth over her face.

With a roar, Louis rushed Alghol. Beth shouted 'No!' but he was lost in fury. Alghol was delighted. '*En Guard! Touché! Torro!*' he crowed. He dodged Louis a few times, then tipped his head back, opened up his shirt and bared his chest. 'Let's see if you dare strike.'

Beth cried again for Louis to stop, but he had no ears for her. He ran forward and lunged. The demon made no attempt to evade the blow. The tip of the knife he was using rammed home against Alghol's stomach with the full force of Louis's run and all his weight behind it. But the weapon just bounced back clean out of his hand.

'Even when he has the courage he lacks the strength. My poor little man. What are you going to do now?' The demon put his head to one side and looked sympathetic. He touched his chest with the tip of a finger; a drop of blood had appeared. 'But you have pierced my sacred skin,' he said. 'And for that you will die.'

He struck Louis in the face hard so that he spun backwards and crashed into the wall where he lay stunned. 'You want to put me back in that box, do you?' hissed Alghol. 'Do you know what's it like in there? You cannot even begin to imagine!'

Shaking his head, he bent down to pick up the bag and looked inside. He took out the brick and smiled. 'To business. But no book. Perhaps you want my part of the bargain? I'm going to let you go? Oh! But guess what? I lied.'

'We never thought you'd keep your word,' said Louis bitterly.

'Nice to die knowing you were right, isn't it?' Alghol smiled. 'You, Louis, are a vessel that needs to be emptied. I think I shall feed you to my girlfriend. But you, Beth. I have other plans for you.'

Beth said nothing; she just watched.

Alghol looked at her tenderly. 'I think you want it too, darling, don't you?' he said. He stepped over to her and took her hand. 'We all need to be loved, Beth – even me. You tried to stop Louis from killing me. A little feeling there already, perhaps?'

Beth cleared her throat. 'I have a deal,' she said.

'I doubt if that will be very interesting.'

'You want to be loved,' she said. 'You were, once.'

Alghol looked closely at her.

'Leah. Remember her?'

The demon was so shocked, he staggered. 'Interesting after all,' he whispered. 'How do you know these things? Ah yes – the mother! Of course. Leah, yes. A long, long time ago . . .'

'Your wife, when you were still alive. She loved you so much. She's waiting for you now,' said Beth. 'You can join her, if you like.'

In an instant the demon had her by the throat. His eyes were glistening. 'How dare you?' he hissed. 'How dare you speak to me like that? How dare you make offers that no one can ever keep?'

'I can keep them.' Beth put her hand to his on her

throat and waited. Slowly he released the pressure. 'I know Glory. I can take you there.'

'No one living can do that.'

'I can take you halfway. My mother can take you the rest of the way.'

The demon stared at her, aghast. 'Is it possible?' he said. 'All these years, I never dreamed it was possible.'

'All the way to Glory. You think you have eternity, Ashur. But this isn't eternity. You alone of all humanity are denied it. I can give it back to you.'

The demon squeezed dreamily on her throat. 'Ashur. No one has called me that for four thousand years,' he said.

His grip had almost cut off her airflow. 'I know who you are,' she gurgled. 'I know what has happened to you. You aren't powerful, Ashur – you're sick. It's a disease. You're trapped for ever in death. I can cure you.'

He stared at her, frowning. 'Cure,' he said. 'You want to cure me of *this*?'

'A door works two ways,' she said. 'You can go back.'

A look of terrible sadness spread across his face. 'Temptress,' he whispered. 'You've come to take me home.'

'What are you scared of?' Beth asked. 'Is it hell?

You're in hell already. Fear and darkness and hunger are all you can ever know. I can satisfy that hunger. I can banish that darkness. I'm offering you a way out.' She lowered her voice. 'Don't you want to know about Leah? She loved you so much! How she cried when you were bitten. And your children. What about them? After all these years . . .'

'How dare you? How dare you?' he whispered. Tears began to form in his eyes.

'She's waiting for you, Ashur . . .'

'No . . .'

'It can stop now . . .'

'Stop it, Beth,' he whispered.

'Don't you want to die, Ashur? Don't you want to touch the light?'

He flung her from him and slammed her against the wall. 'Oh, Ashur, oh, Ashur,' he mocked. 'Do you think I care? After so long?' He touched his tears. 'Do you imagine this is anything but sentiment?'

Beth stood up. 'Ashur . . .'

'Don't call me that!'

'That's who you are.'

'Don't call me that!' he yelled again. He rushed over to her, picked her up and lifted his arm to strike – to kill.

'Leave her,' roared Louis. He had made it back to his feet and was creeping forward. He flung himself at the demon, who stepped slightly sideways and swatted him out of the way again. Louis arched through the air and crashed violently through the conservatory door and onto a bench, smashing it under his weight. He shook his head and tried to crawl forward. Alghol – Ashur – was on the ground, crouching over Beth, stroking her neck. Beth was looking straight into the demon's eyes.

'How often does someone like me come along?' she begged. 'Please, Ashur. Go to the light. Leah is waiting for you. Your children are waiting for you.'

Tears fell from the demon's eyes onto her face. But he shook his head. 'Not this time, dear Beth. I can't let you go. I can't . . .'

He moved her head to one side and, lowering his, put his mouth to her flesh. Beth did not try to evade him. 'Poor Ashur,' she whispered. 'You are too weak to take your chance.' She stroked his hair. The demon let out a single sob and bit down hard. Beth looked calmly over his shoulder at Louis and mouthed to him: 'Strike now.'

Louis picked up a garden fork that he'd knocked over in his fall. He hurried forward as Alghol pulled back from Beth, blood on his lips. 'This is not you – this is not Beth,' the demon hissed. 'Where is her soul? Bring her back – give her to me!' He seized Beth's head in his hands and began to squeeze, but with a convulsive movement, she wrapped her arms round him and held him tight against her.

'Louis,' said Beth, in her mother's voice. 'Come and kill this fucking thing before he finds my daughter in here and turns her into one of them. OK?'

In two steps Louis was at her side. He lifted the garden fork into the air like a spear.

'Let them in!' cried his mother. 'Let them in!'

Louis felt it then; the strength of the dead, thousands of them – all those slain by Alghol who had not turned were with him, in his body, in his arm, with his strength. The demon screamed and tried to pull away, but Beth, too, was armed with the strength of the dead, and he could not move.

'No!' he yelled.

Louis swung the fork down with all his might. He struck sideways, so as not to pierce Beth, and caught the demon in the neck with one tine. It went straight through and out the other side; an arcing spray of blood covered them both.

At the same moment, there were two terrible cries: one, a shriek of agony, came from upstairs, the other was a roar from behind – Ivan. He leaped at Louis with such force that the iron ring in the concrete behind him tore half out. Another leap and the ring tore completely away, and he charged. Louis swung round with the fork and landed a deep blow, right into the shoulder and neck. There was a grim moment while he tugged it away. Ivan howled in pain, and scuttled back out of the way.

Louis turned and brought the fork down again onto Alghol's neck, this time getting two more tines into the flesh, right through and into the wooden floor beneath. He put his foot down on the demon's head and heaved at the fork, but it was jammed tight in the wood. He pulled again, and at the same moment the door to the kitchen burst open and the female vampire, shrieking and screaming like nothing he had ever heard, ran straight at him. Louis let go of the fork and seized her with his hands. He felt as strong as a legion on his own, with all the dead behind him. There wasn't time to deal with her – already Alghol was pushing himself up and jerking the fork, fraction by fraction, out of the wood with his hands. Louis lifted her above his head and stepped to the dining area, where Ivan lay crying and growling at him from under the table. He threw the woman at him; at once, with a terrible fury of snarls, Ivan turned on her. Louis paused only a second to make sure she wasn't going to get away, and then went back to help Beth.

The demon had already forced the fork out of the wood, despite Beth leaning on the fork as hard as she could. Louis snatched it up, and hacked again, this time getting the tines stuck deep in the demon's face.

'The brick, get the brick, quick,' Louis yelled. Behind them, the sounds of the terrible fight between the snarling hyena and the shrieking vampire woman filled their ears. Ivan was tearing her apart lump by lump. With a long groan, Alghol began to force himself again up off the floor, against the pressure of the fork, the blood still pumping from the holes in his neck. He was weakened, but still too strong for Louis to hold back on his own.

'I can't keep him down,' gasped Louis. With one hand, Alghol seized the fork and began to pull it out of his face. There was no way they were going to get the brick in his mouth – not yet.

'Fetch the spade, Beth . . . finish him off with the spade . . .' he groaned.

Beth spotted the spade, lying half in, half out of the conservatory. She grabbed it and returned to the fight, where Alghol had risen to his knees. She ran forward, lifted the spade like an axe, and swung it down on the demon's hand, crushing the wrist and almost severing it. The demon fell to the floor again. Louis dragged the fork out of his face and stabbed again – and again, and again.

At last the creature lay still.

'The brick,' croaked Louis. He looked around,

found it on the floor and bent down, holding it over the creature's mouth. But Beth stayed his hand.

'We can do it now, Louis.' She bent down to Alghol. 'Ashur—' As she spoke, the demon opened one eye, flung out an arm and caught her around the neck. Louis lifted the brick again, about to smash it into his mouth, but Beth stopped him in a choked voice. 'Louis. We agreed – please . . .'

Louis paused. 'Hurry,' he growled. 'Five seconds and then it goes in. You hear me?'

Alghol's mouth opened. He gurgled on blood, then found his voice. 'Agreed,' he gasped. 'Agreed. Send me back.'

Beth gasped a response, but Louis was unable to make it out. 'Let go of her neck! Let her go!' he demanded. But the demon kept up his hold, tight as a vice, forcing her head down towards him, covering his mouth. Beth struggled, but said nothing.

'Do it now,' hissed Alghol. 'I can't go back in the ground. Please . . . send me home.'

'Beth?' said Louis. But she did not reply. 'Let her go!' he screamed.

'She's sending me back . . .' groaned Alghol, muffled by Beth's head on his face.

Louis reached for the fork and stabbed him again – in the chest this time – once, twice, three times. The creature thrashed and screamed, gargling on his own blood – and at last let go. He lay there, quivering from head to foot, but even as Louis watched he could see the flesh knitting together, the skin joining up. He pulled his sister away and picked up the brick.

'Open your mouth now,' he hissed, 'or I'll take your teeth out pushing it in.'

The demon shuddered, and slowly, opening up like a hole in the ground, the jaws parted. They opened up further and further, into a huge, fleshy gash. He cried out, a whimpering sound like the cry of a baby or a puppy dog, that expelled the last of the air in his lungs. Louis rammed the brick home. Then, at last, Alghol lay still.

Coda

It was Christmas Eve, late at night, pitch dark. Beth and Louis were standing in a beech wood on an estate on the edge of the West Yorkshire Pennines. In a place like this, it was the quietest night of the year — perfect for secrets.

At their feet lay three empty graves, with three muddy white cotton bundles beside them. Inside lay Alghol, Ivan, and the remains of the vampire woman that Ivan had torn to pieces. It would have been nice to find a coffin for their friend at least, but that would have made a difficult task harder so they had simply wrapped the bodies in sheets and driven them out here by the flooded quarry to join Don Mayhew for their long, lonely vigil in the ground. In the mouth of each corpse lay an inscribed brick – 'For the living, life; for the dead, the hunger that never ends.'

Beth bent down to one of the bundles at her feet and put her hand on it. 'Sorry, Ivan,' she said. 'We tried.'

His fate for the next few centuries, like that of Alghol and the young woman, was sealed. He would be back, she supposed, at some time or other, but did it really make so much difference? It seemed to Beth, who had caught a glimpse of Glory and understood what it was to be a part of everything, that life and death were not really so far apart. Both entangled the soul in flesh, isolating them from the rest of creation. Her mother and Coll, she hoped, had moved on to Glory and she found it hard not to envy them. For the first time in her life, she was truly alone inside herself, and she felt bereft. The dead made for poor company, but she was beginning to understand that poor company was better than no company at all.

Louis came to stand over the still body of his old friend. 'Sorry, mate,' he said. 'You know I'd rather be out drinking with you, don't you?' He glanced at Beth. 'Want some time to say goodbye?' he asked.

Beth shook her head. Louis tucked her under his arm, and she buried her face in his coat. 'It's not for ever,' he said. 'We can find a cure.'

'Do you think so?'

'We can try. Maybe the answer is there inside you, right now. You're the link. Maybe there's a way of reaching in and pulling them out – you know?'

Beth felt down deep inside her. Where there is a door someone will use it. But what if that someone was herself? Was it possible to open it wide, travel down and find her old lover? If so, perhaps she could bring him back to life or, even better, help him on to Glory. To journey to the land of the dead. What a thing that would be! But she knew from experience how easy it was to get lost down there.

'Better get on,' said Louis. 'Dad's already furious with us for going out on Christmas Eve. Come on . . .'

Louis checked each of the bodies carefully to make sure that the bricks were in place, tied firmly around the back of the head with a chain. Together they pushed them down into the earth and began to shovel soil on top of them.

Beth watched Ivan's undead body disappearing under the dirt. Would he know where he was down there, she wondered? Would he be enraged, or patient, or maddened; or would he just sleep? Beth prayed that he would sleep quietly, until the day came when she found the latch hidden deep inside her that could release him truly and send him on his way.